George Henry Calvert

The Life of Rubens

George Henry Calvert

The Life of Rubens

ISBN/EAN: 9783337226374

Printed in Europe, USA, Canada, Australia, Japan

Cover: Foto ©Raphael Reischuk / pixelio.de

More available books at **www.hansebooks.com**

THE LIFE OF RUBENS.

Heliotype.

Pietro Pauolo Rubens

THE

LIFE OF RUBENS.

BY

GEORGE H. CALVERT.

BOSTON:
LEE AND SHEPARD.
NEW YORK:
CHARLES T. DILLINGHAM.
1876.

RIVERSIDE, CAMBRIDGE:
STEREOTYPED AND PRINTED BY
H. O. HOUGHTON AND COMPANY.

To

THE MEMORY OF MY MOTHER.

CONTENTS.

———◆———

THE LIFE OF RUBENS.

I.

PARENTAGE AND CHILDHOOD.

A LIFE is valuable in proportion as the liver has endowed his fellow-men profitably with himself. To possess powers which, in unfolding and exerting themselves, flow out in good upon one's neighbors, is a mark of superiority. With such powers the genuine artist is especially gifted, and, when he seeks to gratify his delight in the true and the beautiful, he is unconsciously preparing enjoyment and instruction for others, it may be for hundreds of thousands through many generations, — he becomes a perpetual instructor. Before the *Descent from the Cross* of Rubens what multitudes, during more than two centuries, have stood agaze in an admiration which was educating their best faculties? Just before the restitution, in 1815, of the art-treasures which **the**

robber Emperor had gathered into the Louvre
from the churches and best galleries of Europe,
an Antwerp gentleman (one of the commis-
sioners sent to reclaim Antwerp's share) told
me that, go when he would, a crowd larger than
before any other of the great works, even those
of Italy, was always in front of this picture.
Masterpieces of art are like beautiful scenes
in nature, like heroic deeds of men, — we never
tire of them ; for the twentieth, for the hun-
dredth time, we behold them with zest, with a
fresh feeling of elevation.

To the career of Rubens, besides its value
as that of an eminent artist, a unique splendor
is imparted by the richness of his nature.   In
his age he was distinguished for the variety of
his endowments and acquirements, for the fascination and grandeur of his personality.   Like
one of his own eloquent canvases, there was a
brilliancy, a breadth, a sunshine in the man that
made him admirable and attractive to his contemporaries and keep him so for posterity.

The forefathers of Rubens had been for two
centuries denizens of Antwerp, members of
that important class who, as manufacturers,
tradesmen, mechanics, formed in those times
the substance of the population in the numer-

ous and prosperous cities of Brabant and Flanders, and who often played a controlling part in politics. The grandfather of the painter was the first who lifted the family to a higher rank; for, being prosperous and aspiring, he gave his only child and son, John, the best education to be had, sending him finally to Italy, **then** the chief **seat** of learning, where he took, in Rome, the degree of Doctor of Laws in his twenty-fourth year. On his return to Antwerp he married Marie Pypelincx, a lady of good position, distinguished alike for beauty, for intelligence, for elevation of character. In 1561 he became councillor and alderman (*échevin*) **of** Antwerp, a post which he held till 1568. This was the period of the terrible blood-council of **Alva.** Egmont and Horn were beheaded in 1568; and on the 6th of June, Van Straellen, burgomaster of Antwerp, was executed at Vilvorde. John Rubens held the next place in the municipal government, and being denounced, thought it prudent to go into exile with his family at Cologne, where he arrived towards the end of the year.

At that time Cologne was not only the favorite asylum for Flemish refugees, but here for awhile also resided the second wife of the

great Prince of Orange, **Anne of Saxony.**
Anne had quarreled with and separated from
her husband, and was then making appeals to
Alva to get relieved from confiscation those
estates of the Prince of Orange which had been
apportioned as her dower. For conducting her
affairs she employed as one of her agents John
Rubens, who soon obtained her full confidence,
accompanied her on various journeys into Germany, and for whom she took a passionate
fancy, which ended in criminal intercourse.
This being discovered by the Nassau family,
John Rubens was, on one of his journeys,
seized and closely imprisoned in the Castle of
Dillemburg in the Duchy of Nassau.

For three weeks his wife heard nothing from
or of him. At last, in the midst of her growing anxiety, came a rumor of her husband's
arrest, imprisonment, and danger, and right
upon that, letters from himself. With death
hanging over him, — that being there the legal
penalty for adultery, — he wrote to his wife,
confessing his guilt and imploring her pardon.
Here is the answer she sent to her husband.
Seldom does a biographical seeker chance upon
a treasure like this : —

"I could not have thought that you would

impute to me so much resentment. How could
I push severity to the point of paining you
when you are in such affliction that I would
give my life to relieve you from it. Even had
this misfortune not been preceded by a long affection, ought I to show so much hatred as not
to be able to pardon a fault against me, a fault
which is small in comparison with those which
I commit every day, and which make me implore the clemency of Heaven on this condition : *forgive me my trespasses as I forgive
those that trespass against me.* Be then assured
that I have entirely forgiven you: and would
to Heaven that your deliverance depended on
this, for then we should soon be happy again.
Alas! it is not what your letter announces that
afflicts me. I could scarcely read it : I thought
my heart would break. I am so distressed I
hardly know what I write. This sad news so
overwhelms me it is with difficulty I can bear it.
If there is no more pity in this world to whom
shall I apply? I will implore Heaven with
tears and groans, and hope that God will grant
my prayer by touching the hearts of these gentlemen, so that they may spare us, may have
compassion on us ; otherwise they will kill me
as well as you. My soul is so linked to yours

that you cannot suffer a pain without my suffering as much as you.   I believe that if these
good lords saw my tears they would have pity
on me even if they were of stone ; and when
all other means fail, I will go to them, although
you write me not to do so."   The noble woman concludes with these words : ・ " Don't
write again, *your unworthy husband*, for all is
forgiven.   Your faithful wife,

" MARIE RUBENS."

Is it to be wondered at that this woman's
son grew to be a great man ?

To the Prince of Orange, to his brother John
and their mother, she wrote letters eloquent
with the grief of a devoted wife.   Her letters
seeming to have no effect, she went in person,
not to the Prince, who was far away, but to his
mother and brother, Count John, in the neighboring Nassau.

To keep secret the crime of the Princess
was the interest of the Prince of Orange and
his family.   To have proclaimed her guilt, by
enforcing the law against John Rubens, would
probably have alienated Anne's uncles, the
Elector Augustus of Saxony and the Landgrave
of Hesse, whose personal and political support

was at that time (1571) particularly valuable to
the Prince. And, on their side, these royal personages, moved by the dread of family disgrace,
were probably even more bent on concealment
than the Nassaus. Therefore it was given out
that John Rubens had been imprisoned on account of political treason to the Prince of Orange. A rumor reached his wife that under
this pretext he would be secretly made away
with. And there can be little doubt that he
would have been, but for her energetic, high-
hearted course. Marie Pypelincx rose to the
level of the emergency. Appeals to the better
feelings, to sympathy for her, to charitable indulgence (and John Rubens with sad lack of
gallantry had hinted, what was not difficult to
believe, that the first advances had not come
from him), all such petition having proved in-
effectual, Marie being at last even denied ac-
cess to the family, she announced to them that
should her husband suffer death, she, his wife,
would proclaim the cause, and thus defeat the
very object of his destruction. Such a divulge-
ment would, moreover, have further embittered
against the Prince of Orange Anne's uncles of
Saxony and Hesse. At all events, after this
threat things wore a fairer face. Marie was

permitted to visit in his dungeon her husband, whom she had not seen for two years. Soon she induced them to let him out of prison on condition that he should reside at Siegen, a small town of Nassau, she giving money-security of eight thousand gold florins (a large sum in those days), that he would not, without leave, go beyond the walls of Siegen.

The reader will not, I trust, suppose that I am relating this affair merely because it concerns the parents of the great painter, and because such adventures are mostly attractive reading. To be sure, to get at and lay bare the doings and sufferings of the progenitors, especially the immediate progenitors of a man who is remarkable enough to deserve a printed biography, is to throw light upon the character and qualities of the man himself. Yet, to keep proportions, this should of course be done briefly. Whether John Rubens be liberated from prison by being *interné* to Siegen, or by being summarily sent to a better world, bears very indirectly indeed upon the mental composition of my subject, but very directly upon his existence. There needs no conjuror to make known that if John Rubens had been put out of the world in 1572, no Peter Paul Rubens

would have come into it in 1577. But more
than that, in this history of the intrigue of John
Rubens with Anne of Saxony is involved the
settlement of a long disputed point, namely,
where was the great painter born? — a point
deemed of such consequence that four towns,
Antwerp and Hasselt in Belgium, Cologne and
Siegen in Germany, have each claimed the
honor of giving him birth.

In 1568, John Rubens deemed flight from
Antwerp to Cologne prudent, not because he
was a Protestant in religion : that he was not ;
he was a political Protestant, one of a numerous body of Catholics, led by the Prince de
Chimay, who were indignant at the tyrannous
rule of the Spaniards. In his extremity in
1571–72 he asked to have a Protestant clergy-
man, that he might consider with him certain
points of religion and conscience. It was given
out that he had been converted. This was not
true, the conference being a mere show of interest whereby to help appease the anger of the
Prince of Orange and his family. In 1573 the
prison door was opened, and, accompanied by
his heroic wife, John Rubens took a house in
Siegen, retaining, however, at the same time
their domicile in Cologne. In 1574, was

2

born to them a son, Philip, **not in Siegen but
in** Cologne. John **Rubens** had never **ceased**
to be a Catholic, and Marie Pypelincx was
always, in all senses, a good Catholic. Had
Philip come into the world at Siegen and been
there baptized a Catholic, the lie would have
been given, right under the nose of John of
Nassau, to the professions John Rubens had
made of Protestantism. Accordingly his wife
returned to her domicile in Cologne to give
birth to their son Philip.

In 1577 was born Peter Paul Rubens, and
his birthplace is likewise stated to be Cologne
by most biographers **who wrote** prior to the
publication, about forty years since, by Messrs.
Groen van Prinsterer and Bakheuzen **van** den
Brink, of papers preserved at the Hague in the
archives of the Orange family, revealing the
extraordinary episode concerning Anne of Saxony and John Rubens. Since that, the great
painter's place of birth has been transferred to
Siegen. But in 1861, M. B. C. du Mortier, by
a close and shrewd examination of these discovered papers, and a **keen** scrutiny into other
documents, was enabled to issue a pamphlet in
which he proves that Antwerp, the home of the
Rubens family, was also the birthplace of that

member of the family whose renown has made the name historical.

By the *Pacification of Ghent* in 1576, the refugees were allowed to return home and to take repossession of their property, which for so many years had been sequestered. Now, John Rubens was on parole in Siegen, and under heavy bond not to quit that town, and especially not **to cross the** Belgian frontier. He got leave to go as **far as** Cologne, in order to execute there a power of attorney in favor of Marie Pypelincx, her brother and uncle, giving them authority to take possession in his name of all properties to which he was now entitled. This power, executed on the 28th of April, 1577, under the seal of Cologne, is registered in the chancellery of that city. Two months after receiving this power, Marie Pypelincx, on the 29th **of** June, 1577, gave birth to her great son, Peter Paul, so baptized because his birth **fell on** the festival day of Saints Peter and Paul. This were of itself enough to justify the conclusion that Peter Paul was born in Antwerp, whither his mother had gone to execute the power of attorney; but corroborative testimony flows in from several sources. At his **baptism** the **Prince** de Chimay and the Countess Lalaing

were sponsors for the infant, both of them re-
siding in or near Antwerp. Philip Rubens,
born at Cologne, had to be formally naturalized
when in after years he wished to hold office in
Antwerp; whereas Peter Paul, who held a still
higher office, had no need of this formality.
Towards the end of his life Rubens, being engaged to paint a picture to go to Cologne,
spoke of that city as the place where he had
spent the first ten years of his life, but omits
any mention of being born there. When he
was knighted by Charles I. of England he is
called a native of Antwerp.

A short time after Marie Pypelincx went
back to Cologne in 1577, she was enabled to
get permission for her husband to reside per-
manently in Cologne. The Prince of Orange
had remarried, and Anne of Saxony had lately
died.

Would the reader like to see the infant Rubens in the arms of his mother? Let him gaze
at an engraving of Correggio's *Madonna della
Scala.* How happy the two are in each other!
The child's luminous eyes looking cheerily out
into the world, while his arms cling to his beautiful mother. The face of the *Madonna* is too
young for Marie Pypelincx with her sixth in-

fant in her lap ; but, on the other hand, Correggio put into the countenance of none of his
Madonnas the mental force which the history
of Marie justifies us in ascribing to hers. The
child that was to make so strong and high a
flight, and grow into a genially great man,
could not have had a more secure nest than on
the bosom of such a woman. And in his father
he was also happy. John Rubens had had in
his youth the best instruction the times could
give ; had become in difficult circumstances a
trusted magistrate, and now, in the few years
immediately preceding the birth of his illustrious son, Peter Paul, he had gone through
sufferings, dangers, humiliations, which on an
honest stout nature could not but have a chast-
ening influence.

As the boy unfolded into beauty and brightness of body and mind, what may have been
the ideals petted by parental partiality for this
expanding son to fulfill ! None that approached
the one of which the frame was already laid
in his own blooming faculties. Nature, in the
case of an exceptional human being, builds her
immovable foundations so secretly that even
the most loving, aspiring parental wishes cannot
divine the superstructure she intends. Rem-

brandt's father, a prosperous miller, wishing to
give his son a higher career than his own, sent
him to the University of Leyden, thereby to
prepare him for a learned vocation ; but he
soon perceived that the boy had an obstinate
distaste for Latin. He then took him home
again, and finding that, instead of attending to
the business of the mill, he worked at nothing
with zeal but at copying engravings he had
brought with him from Leyden, he consented
to his going back to Leyden to the studio of a
painter.

Rubens had more versatility. From earliest
childhood he learnt readily and willingly whatever task was given him. For the portrait
drawn, in the opening scene of Cymbeline, of
Posthumus, Rubens might have set : —

> " Puts to him all the learnings that the time
>   Could make him the receiver of, which he took,
>   As we do air, fast as 't was minister'd ; and
>   In his spring became a harvest ; lived in court
>   (Which rare it is to do), most praised, most loved ;
>   A sample to the youngest, to the more mature
>   A glass that feated them ; and to the graver,
>   A child that guided dotards."

When first his ear and tongue could distinguish and articulate words, the child Rubens
began to learn three languages, — his mother

always speaking to him in their native Flemish,
his father in Latin, and a tutor in French.

Peter Paul was in his tenth year when his
father died. Marie Pypelincx then quitted Cologne, and with her children went back to her
native Antwerp. Here, under his mother's
watchful eye, the education of Peter Paul was
continued in whatever was then known and
could be taught by the best teachers to an
apt learner. He was probably about fifteen
when the Countess Lalaing took him into her
house as a page. The Countess, his godmother,
and a friend of his mother, probably saw the
bright boy often, and was no doubt fascinated
by his beauty and grace and amiability and
cleverness. To be page in the family of a
noble lady was then deemed a post of privilege
and honor. Young Rubens felt that it was not
suited to him. As much freedom was allowed
to pages, who lived in idleness and luxury, there
could hardly be a place of more dangerous
temptation to a boy, and he beautiful and captivating, just turning toward manhood. A sign
it was, not merely of his being possessed by an
irresistible artistic instinct, but also of sound
moral sensibilities, that young Rubens soon
grew discontented with such a position, and

begged his mother to let him be a painter.
His mother was disappointed. She and his
father had designed and educated him for a
high public career. The vocation of painter
was not then much esteemed. There was not
then in Antwerp, nor indeed had there ever
been, an artist of genius and power to lift it to
its due rank. But Marie Pypelincx was tender
and wise. She called together the members of
her family, and with them the various teachers
who had given her son instruction. The result
of the conference was, that the request of Peter
Paul was granted, and he was entered as pupil
in the studio of a painter.

II.

Our progenitors in Art were the Greeks. Phidias is the æsthetic ancestor of Rubens, as of Leonardo and Raphael. That penetrating, solitary, inextinguishable, magnetic light from Hellas traveled surely on, through obscuration and corruption, to re-illume far distant generations.

Faculty to copy form, with child-like joy in the reproduction, is inborn. Wherever men get to use their hands and fingers, they take to drawing, if only with a stick or stone on the sand, to attempting crude representation of objects, to carving rough images, to imitation of natural forms. All nations show this tendency. In the higher it unfolds itself more variously and fully, until, at a certain period among the highest races, as among the ancient Greeks, there comes from the heaven of genius a flash that kindles the collected intellectual material, and Art is born, to warm, delight, educate mankind.

After Greece had been absorbed into the
Roman State, Greek culture diffused itself
westward, and Greek art planted itself in Rome
and Byzantium. Through the earlier centuries
of our era, Art kept its footing through floods
of barbaric desolation by means of illustrated
manuscripts, missals, pictorial prayer-books,
paintings on the walls of churches and cata-
combs. The tradition was dimly preserved,
the execution was rude; but through the crud-
est, simplest attempts, especially through the
representations of the Madonna and child and
the head of Christ, there soon began to glim-
mer an ideal, some stretching up for a better,
which is the very embryon of Art. The alli-
ance of religion, the aspiration towards unity
with the divine will, gave to Art, in the early
times of its revival, rich nourishment, moving
it to work through the imagination by spiritual
influences, and appealing to every one's feelings
on public occasions. Religion thus gave Art
wings and an atmosphere to soar in.

I believe there are no remains or indications
to show that painting was practiced in Germany or the Netherlands previous to the intro-
duction of Christianity. From Byzantium and
Rome artistic forms and types had been trans-

mitted through unknown hands. Tradition is
an electric line which binds into unbroken
continuity the successive ages of a race, and
preserves from total extinguishment the fire
once kindled by genius. That, through the
innate needs and faculties of the human mind,
Art would have spontaneously come to life in
modern Europe, had there been no Greek tradition and no unearthing of Greek marbles in
the fourteenth and fifteenth centuries, there
can be no doubt. But in that case the heights
gained by the ancients would have been lost
to the moderns. To have antecedent kindred
who created and richly unfolded Art, was a
vantage-ground. The Greeks were the first of
our stock who, through deep sense of the beautiful, gave birth to Art; and to Italians and
Germans it was a privilege to be of their blood,
and thus be able to inherit their wealth.

The founders of the Flemish school of painting were the brothers Hubert and John Van
Eyck. The Van Eycks were men who, standing firmly on the platform raised by their predecessors, were able, on the pinions of genius,
to reach a broader, higher plane, whence they
improved the quality of Art and enlarged its
domain. The origination of a school of paint-

ing in Antwerp may be dated in 1420,—more
than a century and a half before the birth of
Rubens,—when John van Eyck of Bruges, the
first who painted in oil, appeared before the
guild of painters in that city and showed them
a head of Christ done in oil.

In those agitated ages the guilds were important instruments of civilization. They were
an evidence of the virtue there is in sympathetic association. The great Society of St.
Luke was regularly organized in Antwerp in
1442. In that year the supreme magistrate of
Antwerp issued a decree, establishing the number of handicrafts united under the banner of
this Society. Here is the opening of the decree : —

"We, John Vanderbruggen, knight, lord of
Blaesvelt and margrave of the Rhine, burgomaster, alderman and councillor of the city of
Antwerp, make known to every one that the
honest citizens composing the united society of
*painters, sculptors in wood, cutters of stone,
glass-blowers, illuminators, engravers, printers,
booksellers, binders, framers of mirrors, cutters
of images, makers of cross-bows, makers of
panels, painters of glass, goldbeaters, engravers
of figures, manufacturers of boxes intended to*

be painted, potters, curtain-makers, makers of playing **cards**, *upholsterers, box-makers,* and all those who belong to the association of St. Luke, having made known to us that the church-wardens of our Lady of Antwerp have granted to them in the said church a chapel which they have richly ornamented in honor of God and St. Luke, and that they wish to embellish it still more, but are restrained by the fear of seeing their company dissolved, and solicit of us a legal decree, which shall guarantee to them certain franchises, we have to them given and granted," etc.[1]

An æsthetic spirit was the soul of these associations. The guilds of many different towns sometimes met for competitory trials in dramatic or plastic work, in scientific essays or mechanical skill, — meetings which bore resemblance to the Olympian or Isthmian games of Greece. On ceremonial occasions the guilds made the preparations and decorations, the foremost artists doing their best. For the fastuous entry of a prince into Antwerp, Rubens himself executed, in his latter days, some masterpieces, of which engravings are preserved. Of the importance of these guilds, who incor-

---

[1] Alfred Michiels : *Rubens et l'École d'Anvers.*

porated under their many and various **heads**
the most substantial and efficient part **of** the
citizens, a notion may be formed from this,
that the most of them had each a special altar
in some church, which they ornamented, in
rivalry one of the other, with sculpture and
pictures and precious stones. In the Cathedral
of Antwerp there were twenty-four such altars
and chapels, held by different companies.

In those times, accordingly, there was no
lack of painters ; but before 1577 none was
born possessed **of the** generative force and
opulent resources which empower an artist to
make an epoch, to found a **school.** Yet the
Flemish artists **of the** sixteenth century did
a good work. By quite a many-sided cultiva-
tion of painting they mellowed the atmosphere,
which in the fifteenth century was still raw,
and thus did much to create the conditions
needed for the full expansion and free play of
the faculties of the master, whose life-work
was to be the glory of Flanders and Antwerp.
Even the most brilliant and original worker
owes much to conditions. Genius is a flame
which, bereft of **congenial** air, languishes and
expires. The impulsive energetic tempera-
ment, which attends and vivifies the higher

exhibitions of genius, will drive the possessor to movements and doings which, in turn, engender new conditions. Leonardo and Michelangelo and Rubens blew fresh life into the artistic atmosphere of their times.

The first teacher of Rubens was Tobias Verhaeght, a landscape painter. By some, Verhaeght is praised for talent, by others, who have written about Rubens, he is not mentioned. To the belief that he was one of the great master's instructors he solely owes the preservation of his name. Would it be unsound to conclude that his name being remembered is strong presumption in favor of his having been the first instructor of Rubens? The second was Adam van Noort, a man of violent temper, of whom the tradition is, that, to subdue a constitutional melancholy, he was given to strong potations, and that he was never amiable except when through too much drink he was not himself. Van Noort had some name, and was probably a good teacher; for, notwithstanding his rough ways, Rubens stayed with him three or four years.

Incidents are sometimes imagined to suit eminent personages. The great biographies of Plutarch are supposed to be sprinkled with pertinent inventions. **The** following anecdote is easily credible, it fits so well the eager boy, who, unconsciously full of his high destiny under inward momentum, quitted the indulgent fashionable life of a noble lady's page to dedicate himself, through the initiatory drudgery of the studio, to a not yet duly esteemed vocation. It is related that one day, when the master was absent, the pupil took a fresh canvas to try what he could do by himself towards representing a weeping Madonna. He worked for hours, and so intently that he did not hear the returning footsteps of the master, who from behind gazed in admiration **and wonder at his** performance.

From the studio of Van Noort, Rubens passed **into** that of Otto Venius, a better artist and a very different man, learned, cultivated, and kind, and courtly in manners. Otto Venius was born in Leyden, where his father, a man of rank and fortune, was burgomaster, and of such account, that while his son went to Italy to study painting, he was sent on an embassy to the Emperor of Germany. **Otto Venius spent** seven years in Italy, and with profit. **Since the** *Renaissance* it **was the** practice of the most aspiring young painters of the North to steep themselves in the quickening art-atmosphere of the south. A contemporary of Venius, Denis Calvaert, born in Antwerp, became so fascinated with Italy, whither he had gone to perfect himself in landscape-painting, that he made Bologna his home, and grew to be so noted as artist and teacher, that he had many pupils, among them men afterwards so distinguished as Guido, Albano, and Domenichino.

In 1598 occurred a political event which had a bearing on the career of Rubens. Philip II. of Spain, just before his death, transferred the Netherlands to his daughter, Isabella, whom he gave in marriage to the Austrian Archduke Albert. They named Otto Venius painter to the Court. His pupil Rubens, about the same time, being come of age, was received a member of the Society of St. Luke in Antwerp. He had been a diligent student for five or six years. Venius and Rubens had become to each other more like father and son than master and pupil. The teacher warmly appreciated his pupil and admired him without jealousy. In no stinted terms he spoke of the character and talents of young Rubens to the Archduke and the Duchess, who, on his being presented to them by Venius, were so charmed with his in-

telligence, person, and manners, that when he
set out for Italy, — by the urgent advice of Venius, — the Archduke gave him letters to regal personages in Italy. Rubens had already
painted pictures which were admired for their
originality and merits ; among others, according to Descamps,[1] the *Adoration of the Three
Kings*, a *Holy Trinity*, and a *Dead Christ in
the Arms of the Father*, surrounded by angels.

Bidding farewell to his accomplished master
and cordial friend, Venius, and taking a tender
leave of his noble mother, on the 9th of May,
1600, Rubens began what was then a long journey.   He was twenty-three years of age.

[1] Descamps, *La Vie des Peintres.*

III.

CAN we not figure to ourselves the youthful man, radiant with health, strength, beauty, and spirits, aglow with expectation, descending the southern slope of the Alps, his arteries dilated by the lifeful heat, as emerging out of valleys cooled by lively streams and chestnut groves, he rode towards the plains of Lombardy at the end of May. This new light and new shade, this might of sun and affluence of sparkling vegetable life and mineral grandeur, — what a revelation, what a joy to the great eager senses of the young northern giant. Such a teeming, richly colored, illuminated nature was a fit vestibule to the resplendent halls of art he was about to enter. What was this Art? What had the aspiring young student of Antwerp travelled so far to behold?

For students of art Italy had (as it continues to have) a twofold attraction. First, the abundant master-pieces of the great native painters of the sixteenth century; and sec-

ondly, the marvels of **Grecian** sculpture **dug,**
in the fourteenth **and** fifteenth centuries, **out of
the** earth where they had lain buried for **a**
thousand years.

Master spirits, such as were the Italian artists
whom Rubens had come so far to study, were
capable, from innate impulsion, of creating art,
as the Greeks had created it centuries before
the Christian era. The Greeks were not only
the first who created art, but, through their
infallible **sense of** the beautiful, — the matrix
of art, — had unfolded a perfection of human
feature and form, never since surpassed, if
equaled, a perfection the beholding of which
the greatest of the Italians felt to be an education. Standing before these, they were lifted
to an æsthetic platform whence their own pow-
ers gained a sudden freedom and virtue. And
deeper than the transmission of these unpar-
alleled lines and forms through Greek marbles,
may there not have been, was there not, the
transmission of qualities through the blood?
The Greeks **were, figuratively, the** artistic an-
cestors of the Italians; were they not in a large
degree literally their body and soul ancestors?
Southern **Italy was early** colonized by **Greeks,**
and the southwestern part of **the Italian penin-**

sula was called *Magna Grecia.* There must have
been a strong infusion of Grecian blood into the
natives of ancient pre-Roman Italy, who were
already a cognate branch of the one Aryan stock.
Those great-thoughted Etrurians may have been,
most probably were, Pelasgi ; and the Etrurians
were the progenitors of the Tuscans, unquestion-
ably the foremost in mental power of the tribes
of Italy. Besides Dante and Galileo, besides
Cimabue and Giotto, called the founders of Italian Art, Leonardo da Vinci and Michelangelo
Buonarroti sprang from that high race ; and Ur-
bino, the birthplace of Raphael Sanzio, is just
over the eastern border of Tuscany.

Is it not established that before Cimabue
and Giotto, schools of painting under Greek
teachers existed at Sienna and Pisa? Those
irrepressible Greeks !

The three predominating artists of Italy, who,
as it were by one lifelong pull, and a pull all
together, carried art to the lofty height which
has made it the chief glory of modern Italy,
commanded by manliness of character and
largeness of mental power, the respect, the
admiration, the deference, of the loftiest and
best of their contemporaries. They were great
men as well as great artists. To be a great

artist must not a man possess that fullness
and reach and activity of mind which **consti-
tute** greatness? Leonardo, by the **testimony**
of his countrymen, was a masterly engineer,
an inventive mechanician, an admirable musi-
cian and poet, a profound mathematician, architect, sculptor, and painter, with so intense a
sense of the beautiful that the few pictures ex-
tant of his are inexhaustible as studies of every
kind of æsthetic excellence. He is Leonardo
the transcendent. Michelangelo was likewise
architect, engineer, sculptor, painter, and poet;
and by his elevation of character, his genius and
personal dignity, drew to him such regard that
his sovereign, the Grand Duke Cosmo of Florence, rose and took off his hat while he talked
to the sublime worker. On one occasion when,
surrounded by standing cardinals and ambassadors, Pope Julius II. received Michelangelo, he
made him sit beside him. And the youngest
of the marvelous trio, the "divine" Raphael,
who had such facility in reaching the luminous
heights of Art that he **may be** called the supreme, he **so** overflowed with the juices of the
sweetest humanity, that he made himself beloved by all, and disarmed even envy and de-
traction. In his countenance there is such

beauty and gentleness and refinement, that the beholder of his portrait could not surmise the power that lay behind those delicate feminine features, — a power so preponderant, that even the great Leonardo could not resist it ; for, in the latter half of his illustrious career, when he came to Rome he could so little withstand the spell of his young rival's genius — who was his junior by thirty years, — that his works of that period had a Raphaelesque quality.

Beside these three were two belonging to the same predominant class, Titian and Correggio ; and with them others only lower than the highest. This busy, brilliant group covered the walls of palaces and churches with their beautiful creations. In the course of less than a century they lighted Italy up with a new poetry. The genuine artist is a poet with brush in his hand instead of pen.

Through zealous, industrious, quick-sighted study, under good teachers at home, Rubens came rarely equipped with manual skill and technical knowledge. His hands knew how to obey, promptly and faithfully, the minutest and the boldest wishes of his brain. The brain of Rubens possessed, in the highest degree, that most valuable of pictorial gifts, whereby it was

a transfiguring prism to light, untwisting it into
its primitive elements, and then, with an easy
control, recombining them with such harmonious
variety that they delight the eye, like nature's
most ravishing displays of color. Thence he
was drawn first to Venice, eager to behold the
handiwork of the far-famed colorists, Titian
and Giorgione, and Paul Veronese and Tinto-
retto. Here was a harvest and a reaper!

There is only one way for an artist to profit
by the creations of other artists, and that is
through sympathy. A man cannot be an artist
without imitation ; but the faculty of imitation
is comparatively superficial, and he who imitates
without sympathy learns little, if anything, from
his model. From his brother painters the
painter learns as he does from nature, by seizing
the spirit in which they project and accomplish
their work, and this he can only do through
feeling. Without feeling, and much feeling, and
fine feeling, he is a mere artisan, and can only
imitate. An illustration of what feeling is in
Art, in contrast to the mechanical, is given in a
remarkable sentence of "Great Artists and Great
Anatomists," a valuable volume by Dr. R. Knox:
" Hang your drapery not on a machine, but on
a living person of *fine feeling*."

Rubens is said to have copied twenty portraits by Titian. This was done chiefly as practice in *technique*, to get at the method and manipulation of the great colorist. No doubt the young enthusiast (and had he not been an enthusiast he would not have grown to be the Rubens he is) made many copies. This was his best means to get into intimacy with such workers. Hereby he fully grasped their conceptions, got to feel as each one of them felt, while the brush is the carrier between the soul of the painter and the canvas before him. Within himself so strong a spring of power ever bubbled up, that there was no danger to him of closest familiarity with any compeer. The greater the compeer, the more culture he got for his own aspiring individuality. That individuality was too firm and stout to be maimed by any contact, or diverted from its high destination. Raphael in his first works showed that his immediate master had been Perugino, as Rubens that his had been Venius ; but this influence was superficial and temporary, an evidence of that power of assimilation so essential to the due nourishment of æsthetic genius.

How long Rubens remained at Venice is not known precisely ; it may have been a few months or a year. While there he became acquainted with a Mantuan, an officer at the court of Gonzaga, Duke of Mantua. This gentleman took such an admiration and affection for the young Fleming, and on his return home drew so glowing a portrait of him as artist and gentleman, that the Duke invited Rubens to Mantua, and on his arrival received and treated him with favor and distinction. Rubens then presented one of the letters introducing him to Italian princes, which he had brought from the Archduke Albert. To Gonzaga this must have been an enlivening surprise, and to Rubens a proud gratification. Besides being appointed painter to the court, he became a member of the ducal household.

Rubens carried with him everywhere a letter of recommendation written on his countenance and person. Outwardly as well as inwardly nature had endowed him with lavish hand. When he first appeared at Mantua he was in the bloom of young manhood, above the medium height, with a well-knit figure, a broad forehead and superb head, large luminous eyes, a full expressive mouth, topped by a flowing moustache, a rich beard which, like his hair, was brown, silken and curly, with features and con-

tour of rare beauty, an expression **intelligent**
and winning, and a commanding chivalrous air.
All this made up an *ensemble* which captivated
women and won the admiration of men. We
have seen how in childhood he learnt three
languages, Flemish, French, and Latin. To
these he afterwards added Italian, Spanish,
German, and English. One day as Gonzaga
was passing the door of the studio, he was surprised to hear his young friend repeating a
passage from Virgil ; and he was much more
surprised when, on entering and addressing him
in Latin, Rubens answered in the same tongue,
fluently and correctly.

Petty Italian sovereigns were often in that
age the chief fosterers **of** art and letters, and
among them Gonzaga was conspicuous for liberality and appreciation. As a cordial, intelligent
friend, whose friendship was valuable to **the**
young Flemish painter, the Duke of Mantua en-
gages our interest ; and therefore, very welcome
is a sketch given of him in a volume published
at Madrid in 1874, by M. Cruzada Villaamil,
entitled " Rubens, Diplomatico Español " :—

" In the beginning of the seventeenth century
the Duke of Mantua was Vincent I. of Gonzaga,
born in 1563, the son of William the Hunchback

and Eleanor of Austria. From his father he
inherited neither the bad shape of his body nor
the economical dispositions of his soul. A man
of lordly bearing, and lavishly expensive, he
stinted himself in no enjoyment, and squandered
the hoard accumulated by his father, as much
by free, licentious living as by giving countenance and aid to learned men, artists, and poets,
and forming a rich museum of objects of art.
Galileo and Tasso and Rubens were of the
number of those who enjoyed his bounty, and
the museums of London and Madrid bear witness to the wealth of his collection. Actresses,
and pretty women of all classes and conditions,
made his life a series of adventures as scandal-
ous as exciting, and more like fictitious tales
than actual occurrences. With truth it may be
said, that no prince of his time lived in more
splendor and sumptuous magnificence, carrying
every kind of luxury and enjoyment to an almost
incredible excess."

It may be thought that the intimacy of such
a patron would be more dangerous than serviceable to a handsome, captivating young man.
In quitting the Countess Lalaing, Rubens had
given a hint of the stuff there was in him. He
was now master of the technical knowledge he

had resigned the pageship to acquire, and found himself in the best condition for turning this knowledge to account, and, by studying the gems among the Duke's pictures and antique marbles, for accomplishing the object of his journey to Italy. Moreover, the liberal Duke set him to creating original works. There was no frivolity in Rubens. He was not to be drawn from a deliberate, serious purpose by superficial temptations. His high destiny depended on his solidity of mould as much as on his genial gifts.

On his part, Gonzaga must have had a certain elevation of nature, and no ordinary insight, to value a young stranger who had yet his renown to achieve. For what he did for Rubens he was repaid at the time by his own feelings, and again, in a way not dreamt of by him, by the feelings of a remote generation, who, towards the end of the nineteenth century, honor him as the substantial friend of Galileo, of Tasso, of Rubens, and who thereby save the name of Gonzaga from the oblivion into which have fallen so many of the princes, his contemporaries.

IV.

FOR their adherence to Charles V. in his Italian wars, the rulers of Mantua had by that emperor been created Dukes of Mantua and Marquises of Monferrat. To continue to be on good terms with the powerful house of Austria, the chief of which was the King of Spain, was still the interest of a small state like Mantua, her territory being where it was, bordering on that of Milan, then a province of Spain. Whether or not there was, about this time, any misunderstanding between the two courts, which it was of course the Duke's policy to remove, or whether he was merely prompted by an habitual feeling of deference and good will towards Spain, and by the opportunity which its indulgence gave for his love of lavish display, whatever the motive, he determined to send costly presents to Philip III. and to the Duke of Lerma, his powerful favorite, and to make Rubens the envoy to deliver them. The having in his service so accomplished and superb a cavalier may have been one of the

incentives to the measure, the fitness of the
young Flemish painter for such a duty being so
conspicuous. Moreover, Gonzaga had in his
Museum a series of portraits of beautiful women, and Rubens was just the man to enlarge
it by additions from Spain.

Thus did Rubens have greatness thrust upon
him in a way that might have prevented him
from achieving greatness, had he not been born
great. Liking, as great colorists, it has been
said, are apt to like, to make a brilliant appearance, and not averse to worldly consideration,
he yet never allowed secondary gratifications
to traverse the primary aim of his efforts, the
high purpose upon the compassing of which he
deeply felt that the full enjoyment of his being
depended. The mission to Spain was an invit-
ing opportunity for his art.

Behold him then, on the 5th of March, 1603,
attended by a numerous suite, riding out of the
western gate of Mantua on his way to embark
at Genoa with his precious cargo. This cargo
consisted of a "gorgeous coach and seven
beautiful horses, twelve arquebuses, six of
whalebone and six variegated, and a vase of
rock crystal filled with perfumes, for the King
of Spain. For the Duke of Lerma, a number

of pictures, a silver vase **of large dimensions** inwrought with colors, and two **vases of gold.** **For** the Countess of Lemus, a cross and two candelabra **of rock crystal.** For the Secretary, Pedro Franqueza, two vases of rock crystal and a complete set of damask hangings, the edges of gold tissue." Rubens disembarked with his treasures at Alicante, April 23d.

The King was expected at Valladolid. From Alicante to Valladolid was a long journey in those days of slow travel and bad roads. **On** the seventeenth **of** May, Rubens **writes from** Valladolid to the Duke's Secretary.

"After twenty days **of travel, tedious** on account of continuous **rains** and great winds, we **arrived** on the thirteenth of May at Valladolid, **where** Sigr. Annibal Iberti [the Minister of **Mantua**] received us with the greatest courtesy, although he told me that the orders of his sovereign lord had not yet reached him. To this announcement, which much surprised me, I answered that I knew with certainty **what was** the intention of his Highness, and that to say **more would** be superfluous, **after** so many examples to show **that I was** not the first who **had come addressed to him in this** same manner. **Perhaps Iberti had his** reasons for talking to me in this fashion. He continues to be very good and kind to me, and has begged me to write all this to your lordship."

On the same day he wrote to the Duke himself, to give information of his arrival and that of the horses, which he tells him, "are in as good condition and as handsome as if they had just come out of the stable of your Serene Highness." The attendants were in good health, except the *valet de chambre.* The vases of rock crystal he brought with him. The other things were following after. He hopes to fulfil completely the instructions given him by his Highness : "and if on account of the excessive expenses, or from some other cause, any action of mine shall have such an appearance as to displease your Highness, I beg and implore you not to condemn me until I shall have been permitted to prove its unavoidable necessity. Meanwhile I will seek comfort in the elevation of your Highness' judgment which is equal to the nobleness of your heart, before whose serene brightness, I bow with respect, kissing your noble hand.

"From Valladolid, on the seventeenth of May in the year 1603. From your Highness' humble servant.   PETER PAUL RUBENS."

These passages are from the volume by M. Villaamil, *Rubens Diplomatico Español,* and apparently not written in Spanish by Rubens, but translated from his Italian by M. Villaamil. In that age the address of subalterns to superiors blossomed with the gaudiest flowers of rhetorical hyperbole.

And now came trouble from a quarter not suspected. The cases when opened at Alicante were found to be in excellent condition, but when the contents were taken out at Valladolid, the pictures had suffered deplorably, as is seen by the following letter from Rubens to Sr. Annibal Chieppio, secretary to the Duke of Mantua.

"Unjust fortune, jealous of my great satisfaction, cannot resist, according to her wont, to mar my joy with some mishap. The pictures, packed under my direction and watchfulness with all imaginable care in presence of the Duke himself, when opened in Alicante by order of the custom-house officers, were in a perfect state of preservation ; now, when unpacked in the house of Sr. Iberti, they seem to be literally ruined, to such a degree that I despair of being able to get them into order. The canvases themselves, although provided with

metal guards and inclosed in double lining,
have rotted under the effect of rains, incessant
for twenty-five days (a thing never known before in Spain) ; the colors have peeled off, and
through the uncommon dampness are puffed
out, which in many places is irremediable, unless they are scraped with a knife and fresh
color laid on. Such in plain terms is the evil,
which I do not exaggerate, in order not to give
occasion for any one believing that I wish be-
forehand to give value to their restoration,
which I shall make in every possible manner ;
thus accomplishing the task given me by his
Highness to transport with care works of other
painters, among which there is not a stroke of
mine. I speak thus, not from resentment, but
à propos to the wish of Sr. Iberti, who desires
that with the assistance of Spanish painters, I
should paint at once a number of new pictures.
This I do not approve, considering the short-
ness of the time at our disposition, together
with the incredible incapacity and idleness of
these painters, and their manner of painting,
absolutely distinct from mine. In short, *per-*
gimus pugnantia secum cornibus adversis com-
ponere. Moreover, the fact could not be con-
cealed, as these very painters, despising my

collaboration and my directions, would cry out against usurpation and proclaim that the work was all theirs. Besides, I have resolved never to mix myself with another, even if he were a great man ; and a work done in this way is as much that of one as of the other, and for my part I should find myself robbed, which would be very unsatisfactory in a work of so little importance and unworthy of my name, which is not unknown here."

Knowing, as we now do, what a right Rubens had to a healthy pride, we enjoy the stout utterance of it in this letter. He here shows himself, too, what he always was, the energetic clear-headed man of business. As to his contemptuous expressions towards the Spanish painters, it must be borne in mind that in 1603 Velasquez was a child four years old, and Murillo not yet born. It may be of interest to note, that in 1603, while Rubens was at the opening of a brilliant career, Shakespeare was at the height of his dramatic success ; that Queen Elizabeth lay on her death-bed while Rubens was making the voyage between Genoa and Alicante ; and that during this summer the young Genoese Spinola took command of the Spanish army in the Netherlands to carry on the famous siege of Ostend, and confront (proving himself worthy to confront) the greatest captain of the age, Prince Maurice of Orange, son of William the Silent and Anne of Saxony, that Anne who, by her love for John Rubens and its consequences, put in jeopardy the existence of Peter Paul Rubens.

With his habitual diligence and rapidity Rubens wrought at the restoration of the damaged pictures, having to reject several as incurable, and supplying their place with two fresh ones by his own hand, a *Democritus* and a *Heraclitus*, both life-size; so that the rain which had threatened the destruction of the chief present to the Duke of Lerma, turned to a rare benefit, being the cause of his becoming the possessor of two originals by the hand of Rubens in place of several copies of celebrated Italian masters, for such were all sent by Gonzaga. This good fortune of the two Dukes, the giver as well as the receiver, was owing to the signal efficiency, the fidelity and ableness of the young envoy, who, in the readiness and fulness of his resources, exhibited that mastership which can convert a misfortune into a gain, a mastership which needs not always a large field for its display.

Copies even of the finest gems, unless done by a hand as cunning as that which wrought the marvelous originals, are not a very regal offering.   Mostly, their deserved fate is banishment to the garret.   To the powerful Duke of Lerma they were an appropriate gift, he having mistaken them for originals.   From the continued decadence of Spain under his premiership, it is not unjust to infer that he knew more about painting than about statesmanship.   The King, Philip III., son of the famous and infamous Philip II., was little else than a big, indolent, petted baby.   He was delighted with his new toy, the coach and six.   The beauty, distinguished manners and sprightliness of the envoy from Italy, the King and his court were capable of admiring; but probably, so long before the maturity of Valasquez, the artist Rubens, was not more deeply seen into than was, in that same summer, Shakespeare by his new King and followers.

Besides the two pictures, already mentioned, rapidly executed to fill up chasms in the present to the Duke of Lerma, Rubens painted an equestrian likeness of the Duke himself, and portraits of some of the court ladies for Gonzaga's gallery of beauties.   He probably painted

others on this first visit, as more than one
hundred and twenty pictures by him are known
to have existed in Spain. With Rubens it is
more difficult than with most leading masters
to distinguish always his earlier from his later
work. A discouraging fact is that of these
hundred and twenty, not more than sixty are
left, the others having disappeared and per-
ished in various ways.

By the King and his favorite, Rubens was
loaded with presents. Kings and Grandees
must make presents, and munificent presents;
however empty the exchequer, their overtop-
ping position and exceptional dignity demand
full hands. The King of Spain's soldiers in
the fatal Netherlands were unpaid and unclad;
his treasury was chronically famished; his people, — crushed between the upper and nether
grindstones of sacerdotal and monarchic ab-
solutism, — were in a state of moral and intellectual atrophy. The gifts from the Duke of
Mantua might justly be looked upon as political
tribute, to be returned in political protection;
but the Duke's envoy, the captivating painter,
must carry away with him deep and grateful
impressions of royal and noble bounty.

On this first visit Rubens was in Spain about

a year. The Duke Gonzaga wished him to return by way of France, in order that he might
paint for the Mantuan gallery of beauties some
ladies of the Court of Henry IV. The showy
Duke, a man apparently of much surface in
proportion to his depth, probably thought that
by the personality of Rubens an effect as
marked as that on the Court of Spain would
be produced on the Court of France, and that
to be so splendidly represented would add to
his own importance there. Rubens, not deem-
ing a charge like this very elevated, and being
intent on his art, disliked the scheme, and to
the Duke Gonzaga's secretary, who had urged
it in a letter to him, he wrote very distinctly
and independently of his repugnance. He did
not return by way of France, but, as he had
come, by sea.

The purpose for which Rubens had been
sent had, owing to his artistic skill and personal qualities, been most successfully accomplished ; he had enjoyed opportunities for enlarging his knowledge and for deepening his
acquaintance with men ; and at the Court of
Spain he left a name which was to be of value
quarter of a century later, when he revisited that
country on a much more important service.

V.

RUBENS was always a student. With the best minds 't is ever thus. Their waking hours, when not busied with execution, are given to gathering and revolving and adapting. A warm genial nature is assimilative, and finds food everywhere. When intent upon and absorbed into a subject, the man of genius knows how to make subservient to his end circumstances and objects apparently indifferent and even adverse. For the offspring that he is inwardly nursing he sucks juice out of the stars and the earth and manifold man. When Rubens was at work on one of his great canvases, a walk or ride into the air would replenish him with tints, with effects of chiaroscuro, with lines of grace or meaning, with glances of expression in passers, with hints of beauty or power.

It is not every man who can study; and most of those who can, that is, who can classify facts, and trace effects to causes, and take in principles through steady contemplation,

study by fits. The thoughtful man of genius
is a perpetual, an incessant student. Nature
and history, in all their variety, their calm and
tempest, their beauty and grandeur, are ever
alive to his apprehension or his consciousness,
cultivating his faculties, deepening his insights.
Rubens, well taught and trained by capable,
responsible parents, continued his education
through life ; and all the knowledge that he
acquired, his acquaintance with Latin literature, as well as that with Greek sculpture and
mythology, his intercourse with men of diverse
ranks and countries, all fed his art, not only
giving it variety in subject, but helping it to
breadth and depth and truthfulness. When
Art is thus followed, the artist making most
things without and within tributary, it sufficeth
to the largest, strongest nature, filling his being
delightfully.

Philip Rubens, the nephew and first biogra-
pher of the painter, says of his uncle, " He
never gave himself the pastime of going to
parties where there was drinking and card-
playing, having always had a dislike to such."
Rubens did not need to look about for means
to "kill the enemy ;" he needed no pastimes ;
his mind was too full and earnest. He rested

his faculties by alternations of employment, laying down his magical pallet to take up a good book, or to review his antique marbles and gems, or to have a good talk, or a gallop on a mettlesome horse. Drinking and gambling are the resource of the one-sided, or the wrong-sided, or the empty who have not head enough to keep them busy, or of the victims of social and industrial insufficiency. They are an abuse of nature, unfailingly punished; for nature is an inexorable retaliator. The attempt to make hour-long entertainers of life, appetites which are purely its subordinate feeders, ends always in disappointment and perversion. The organization of Rubens was too high-strung and full-strung for such abuse. He was too clear and clean to subject himself to the usurpation of habits which are attended by intellectual distraction and moral impairment. These words of Philip refer to his uncle in maturity, in his happy home. We should like to know how the young bachelor spent his evenings in Mantua.

As Gonzaga was now past forty, it is charitable to suppose that he had sown his wild oats. Would Rubens have remained an inmate with him so long, would he have come to look

on Mantua, as he calls **it** in a letter from Spain,
as his adopted country, had the court of the
Duke not been well ordered? The man who
had elevation and discernment to admire and
favor Galileo and Tasso and Rubens, was likely
to have about him men of culture and character. There was not at Mantua for Rubens, as
there was at Correggio for Allegri (though in
the latter part of his short, productive life), a
Veronica Gambara, whom Count Pompeo Ghe-
rardi calls, "cultivator of letters, a poetess of no
common merit, a good wife, exemplary mother,
wise in the government of Correggio, discreet,
charitable." That indeed would have been,
even for Rubens — so favored through life —
an alarming partiality of fortune, had he found
in Mantua another high lady patroness, he who
in the Infanta Isabella had so cordial a one at
Brussels. We have no report of what the
Duchess of Mantua was. She may have been
a solid, serviceable friend to Rubens, and may
have had about her ladies like herself, who
could sympathize with as well as admire the
brilliant, aspiring artist; and more than their
admiration the sympathy of women is healthily
stimulating to a man of genius.

Rich exuberance of life in Rubens was con-

trolled **and** guided by a high, definite purpose,
and a bracing will. His ardent activity required
that he be at work wherever he was. To Italy
he had come to do an elevating work, which
could be done nowhere else, and that was to
put his own soul in direct close communion
with the souls of some of Italy's chief workers.
So competent a pupil the great masters of Italy
had not then had, or since. While studying
these in the intimacy of reproduction, copying
their best, so much native power had he, **that**
by their power he could not be dazzled **or** overcome to voluntary or involuntary imitation.

Among the pictures in the Duke's collection
were several by Mantegna, — one of the earliest
and topmost in that bloom of productiveness
which, a hundred years before, had of a sudden
perfumed Italy with the poetry of pictorial art,
— and who, be it here stated for the honor of
all concerned, had been called from Padua, his
birthplace, to Mantua by an ancestor of Gonzaga, moved by the same feeling of sympathy
with genius which had made the present Duke
offer to Rubens so generous and profitable a
hospitality. In copying one of **a** series by this
master, called *The Triumph of Cæsar*, Rubens,
in place of a sheep walking **by** the side of an

elephant, put in a lion growling at the elephant, who raises his trunk to strike the lion. Especially characteristic was this, showing the confidence and boldness of his hand which could take such a liberty with an admired master, and giving at the same time evidence of the bent of his genius, which delighted in movement and action, in the play of power.

To make copies for Gonzaga, Rubens had been to Rome before he was sent to Spain ; for in a letter to the secretary, written in Spain, among objections to the proposal to return through France, he cites Rome as an illustration of how much longer time was needed to perform the tasks committed to him than had been at first estimated, weeks stretching into months. While at Rome, during his second visit probably, he executed a commission given him by the Archduke Albert, to paint three pictures for the Church of Santa Croce di Gerusalemme, connected with which the Archduke, before his marriage with the Infanta Isabella, had formerly borne the Cardinal's hat. "These pictures," says Dr. Waagen, "represented the *Crowning with Thorns*, the *Crucifixion*, and the *Finding of the Cross*, and were remarkable as specimens of his style of painting at that period. They were brought to England in 1811, and sold by auction the following year."

Could we but go along with Rubens when he went to the Sixtine Chapel! Had we just one letter from him to his mother, or to Otto Venius, relating his first interview with the majestic creation of Michelangelo! What was his thought when he looked on the grand recumbent form of Adam, so instinct with power and grace, or some others of the colossal figures which make of the ceiling of the Sixtine the highest achievement of pictorial effort, — forms the sight of which lifted even the supreme Raphael to a higher level, and before which all genuine artists stand in reverent admiration. To the great eager eyes of Rubens this vast work was comparatively fresh, not having been yet desecrated by dust and cobwebs and the smut of candle-smoke. In fellowship with such grandeur how his large breast must have swelled!

All those marvels of conception and execution Rubens could take in at once. A copious, potent man can only be clearly judged, be fully prized, by his peers. The most cordial grasp of genius none are permitted to share but those

who have near consanguinity with genius ; and
with his most fiery puissant sons there needs
besides, for complete valuation, equality of calibre. Since the death of Raphael, no peer of
the creator of the Sixtine frescoes had stood
before them until the day that the young Fleming looked his fill in their sublime presence.
In such a beholder, such a sight awakens a
new consciousness of power : it gives a fresh
impulse to elements not before fully moved.

It is related, that in the beginning of Michelangelo's work on the vault of the Sixtine Chapel, he being absent one day, Bramante, who
had the keys, took Raphael in to show him
some of the first finished heads. A short time
afterwards Michelangelo, on coming out of the
studio of Raphael, said to his companion,
" Bramante has been showing Raphael my
heads." The moment his young rival beheld
them, he seized their new significance, and had
the genial strength of perception to accept
them at once as an advance in art.

To the *Last Judgment*, painted by Michelangelo on the perpendicular wall of the Sixtine
Chapel, Rubens was attracted by the vitality
of vehement movement, the boundless variety
of muscular contortion, — especially attracted,

because of his kinship with the joy his great Italian predecessor had in such energetic bodily exhibition, and his power to multiply attitudes. The contemplation bore rich fruit. In the Munich Gallery are two large pictures by Rubens, one a *Last Judgment*, and one a *Fallen Angels*, besides two small pictures on the same subjects. The smaller *Fallen Angels*, Sir Joshua Reynolds declared, is "one of the greatest efforts of genius that Art has produced."

The Pope, Paul V., was so much charmed with Rubens, that he wished to retain him in Rome. Whilst there he painted pictures for the Pope and for several Cardinals and princely houses. He had the extreme gratification of having his brother Philip join him, in company with whom he diligently studied the antiquities of Rome. In 1608, the result of their researches was published by Philip in a volume, to the literary part of which Peter Paul contributed, besides giving the drawings for six copperplate illustrations.

Wishing to study the best products of each of the schools of Italy, Rubens passed from Rome to Florence. Here, as elsewhere, owing to the letters of Archduke Albert, confirmed by his brilliant personal qualities, he was favor-

ably received by the Grand Duke Ferdinand I.,
and by him was engaged to paint several pictures, among them a *Hercules between Venus
and Minerva.* Hercules was a favorite subject with him. In Spain he executed a series,
called *The Labors of Hercules*, besides three
separate ones, representing the slaying of the
Dragon, the struggle with Antæus, and the
combat with a lion. Lions were always welcome to Rubens; and a single canvas whereon
he could set forth in one view the gigantic muscular force of Hercules, swollen to its utmost
by attack and defence, and the terrible grandeur
of leonine rage, he could not but work at with
a rare rapidity and enjoyment.

To Rubens we owe the snatching from total
destruction of the celebrated cartoon of Leonardo da Vinci, called *The Battle of the
Standard*, he having carefully copied, while at
Florence, the only remnant of it then surviv-
ing. Of the pictures he painted in Florence,
the one now most valuable is his own likeness,
for the priceless Grand Ducal collection of self-
painted heads of artists. This is the portrait
so often copied and engraved; a two-third view
of the face, with the low, broad-brimmed hat
worn on one side, after the fashion of the day,

exposing the rich curly hair above and behind
the ear, the golden acorn and short tassel of
the hatband peeping over the rim just above
the eye most in shadow, round the neck a laced
ruffle and gold chain, — a picturesque portrait,
whose strong, roomy brow and head, large tran-
quilly shining eyes, expressive mouth, regular,
but animated contour and features, present an
impressive, most attractive countenance to the
beholder, who, while looking at it, readily ac-
cepts the reports of the fascination exercised
by the original over those who approached him.

On the way north from Florence, Rubens
stopped at Bologna, where the Caracci were
then at their height, Annibale, the foremost of
them, not having died till the year after Rubens
quitted Italy. The Caracci, through native
force, somewhat revived decadent art, resisted
and confounded the mannerists of their generation, men aiming to produce the effects of
the great masters (who culminated in Raphael)
by imitating their external characteristics ; as
though corpses, wrought into attitudes, could
do the work of bodies moved by souls. Without inwardness, and deep inwardness, nothing
genuine and permanent can be achieved in
art. Even good qualities and aptitudes are not

enough : there must be a strong individuality, so strong, that the man is moved to work as artist because he feels that he has something to set forth that has not been set forth before, something in itself new, or, new aspects of the old. The painter of pathetic or heroic subjects must feel with his personages, must have sensibilities so rich and fresh as to be able to transport himself into them, and paint his picture from within. He must dive into his own soul ; and, to bring forth on a high plane anything excellent, he must have a soul deep and large enough to dive into. But, as Goethe says : " Rarely does it occur, especially in these later times, that the artist is able to penetrate into the depth of his own soul, as well as take the measure of outward objects, and thus, instead of producing works of a merely superficial effect, emulate Nature herself, and create a spiritually organic whole, giving to his work an import and a form, that make it seem at once natural and supernatural." [1] And again, in the same essay : " The spiritual elaborates the subject with reference to its inward relations, discovers the subordinate motives, and,

[1] *Essays on Art*, by Goethe : translated by S. G. Ward, Boston, 1845.

as the choice of subject furnishes in general
the best criterion of the depth of artistic feeling, so the development of motives is the
measure of its richness, breadth, fullness and
refinement."

But in Art, as in Literature and Science,
the spiritual, — sometimes under specious dis-
guises and pretexts, — is liable to invasions
from and submersions under the material. Every now and then it seems needful to resteep
humanity in the material, in order to broaden
man's hold on the earth.

Rubens had no motive for tarrying long in
Bologna. There was nothing, peculiar to Bologna, for one of his calibre to study. The
Caracci, like a few others, made an oasis
around them in the desert of contemporary
Italian art; but they were not men of broad
creative genius. Had there not been artists
far greater than they, Rubens would never
have traveled to Italy. From Bologna he proceeded to Milan. As during his long stay in
Italy, Rubens spent several years at Mantua,
he of course visited neighboring Parma, and
could not but, from the focus of his admiration,
snatch some kindling sparks; for Correggio
was great enough to give congenial hints to

the greatest. The chief treasure of Milan, that
before which, as a display of human genius and
executive faculty, beholders rise to their best
mood, is the *Last Supper* of Leonardo da Vinci,
the renowned *Cena*, painted in the refectory of
a convent. It was then in its wholeness and
comparative freshness, not having been yet
blasted by barbarism, damp, and antiquity.
One could believe that Rubens, after a first
devouring look, such as only artists can give,
in the flood of his admiration dropped on one
knee in presence of this marvelous masterpiece.   Here was that magical plastic achievement, the transference of the worker's soul into
his work, the incarnation of elevated conceptions by means of powers at once the broadest
and most exquisite.   Leonardo da Vinci was a
penetrating, ceaseless searcher into his inmost ;
and therein lay such jewels, that all through
his life he kept bringing up one after the other,
of divers kinds, treasures, at whose value and
beauty the world continues to wonder.

Rubens made a copy of the *Cena*, as he had
done of the *Battle of the Standard.* He doubtless felt that the difference in the action of
their faculties, between himself and Leonardo
made the study of this transcendent mind par-

ticularly serviceable to him. Like Raphael and
Michelangelo, **Rubens** not only worked rapidly,
but finished **quickly.** His means **put** themselves forth with readiness ; he did not brood
over a picture. He knew how to make the
invisible present through the visible ; **but** the
beholder takes it all in **without postponement,**
at least the broad effects ; **he goes away** satisfied. **He comes back again** and again **for**
re-enjoyment ; **but at each time his enjoyment**
completes **itself.** Not so, **Leonardo. In a**
countenance of his there is more of the depth
and mystery **of** humanity. In standing, no
matter how often, before that figure with the
crosier, in the Louvre, said to be a St. John,
you are enchanted, but somewhat baffled. Upon a face, Leonardo concentrates his whole
self, putting the thought **of many** into one.
Hence he left so few pictures. **Rubens** diffuses
himself easily over many figures, each one suit-
able, admirable **in** color, attitude, and expression, **but** none subtly suggestive, seldom drawing you into the impenetrable.

When Ludovico Sforza, Duke of Milan, re-
proached Leonardo with not working more
steadily and faster at the *Cena*, Leonardo answered him, that artists never work so hard as

when they seem to do nothing, great thoughts shaping themselves in the laboratory of the brain ; and that often a painter does more with his arms crossed than when he has the brush in his hand. A characteristic answer. The brain, indeed, of every great painter is such a laboratory, where work is prepared for the canvas, and pictures are wrought, blushing with virgin life, pictures that are more distinct to the creative artist's eye than the corporealities about him, and than his own finished handiwork. Nay, in order that he attain to excellence, his mind should be so poetically imaginative that he looks at what is bodily present with a visionary eye. Raphael declared, that with the most beautiful model before him he could not approach the excellence of nature, unless he carried within his thought an ideal beauty to help him. Hence it is that, to ordinary realities, the poetical mind always adds tints that freshen them ; or rather, the poetical mind sees deeper into the reality, and reveals its hidden qualities and possibilities. Now, in Leonardo, this upreaching after perfection, this yearning for beautiful possibilities, was peculiarly intense, so intense that he could not satisfy himself. Like our own Allston, his visions were so spiritual and beautiful, that he could not fully incarnate them with his material instruments. After painting for four years on his celebrated *Mona Lisa* he desisted, saying, it was yet unfinished. Rubens took time, no doubt, for his celebrated *Chapeau de Paille*, but not the tenth of that. Leonardo, who lived many years longer than Rubens, did not probably leave more than a hundred pictures ; Rubens left more than a thousand. Does any one exclaim, Would that Leonardo had painted more and Rubens fewer? Beware of laying hands on men of exalted genius : such hands are profane. Accept with silent thanks what they bequeath that is good and noble : give not even a tear to their sorrows, for these were an essential part of their puissant being. This of seizing hold of the infinite with our finite wishes is a very silly, sad proceeding.

The last and, except Mantua, the longest station of his æsthetic tour, Rubens made at Genoa. Here he was preceded by a trumpet-tongued imposing herald, his fame. By the eulogies which, for several years, had been multiplying and strengthening from other cities of Italy, the Genoese were prepared to receive him with enthusiasm. Nobles, princes, mer-

chant-princes vied with each other in doing
him honor and giving him orders. Besides
painting many pictures, he made sketches of
the fronts of the most remarkable palaces and
churches of Genoa, with drawings of their
plans and sections and elevations,—a congenial labor, done so thoroughly that a few years
later he published the result in a volume illustrated with one hundred and thirty-nine copperplate engravings. On the title-page is the
design of a sitting hen, and above it as motto :
Noctu incubando diuque, than which surely no
other could be more appropriate to Peter Paul
Rubens, an unceasing worker night and day.

In the beginning of November, 1608, he
learnt that his mother was ill. He at once set
out for Antwerp.

VI.

RUBENS never again saw on earth his noble mother. She died while he was on the way from Genoa. On reaching Antwerp he shut himself up in the Abbey of St. Michael's, where her remains had been buried, and continued there in seclusion for three months. She was one whose loss was to be deeply grieved by such a son. He knew and felt what a mother she had been to him, and he could value her uncommon worth as a woman. On the monument he erected to her he inscribed an epitaph, beginning *Maria Pypelingia prudentissima lectissima femina*, which may be translated, wise and rare woman. In such epithets there was no overcharging by filial piety.

On getting back to Antwerp from Italy Rubens felt somewhat as Goethe felt on getting back to Weimar. He at first was sad with a longing for the sunny South. Goethe had passed eighteen months, Rubens eight years, in Italy ; had there been honored, feasted, and, above all, appreciated, sympathized with. And how was he to live without the daily companionship of Michaelangelo, Raphael, Titian, Leonardo, and their followers.

Rubens was now, at the age of thirty-one years, a painter of European renown; for his mastership in Art had been acknowledged loudly by Princes and Nobles and Popes; and in that day the favor of these was fame. But what is of still greater significance and of lasting importance, in Italy he had astonished the soberest judges by works, and they not few in number, which took their place, without obtrusion, in Italian Churches and Palaces beside the splendid master-works of that land, teeming as no other, in modern times, had teemed then, or has since, with pictorial genius and power. When after an absence of eight years, and eight most industrious and profitable years, Rubens retrod the soil of his native Flanders, he was a new glory added to his country. And yet he was dispirited. He missed the mental atmosphere he had been breathing so long, that the sudden deprivation of its stimulus left him low in tone, and he felt that he must go back to dear Italy.

We have seen how Rubens had been, not

only honored, but intimately prized by sov-
ereign and controlling personages in Italy.
And now from the Duke of Mantua he received pressing invitations and honorable ad-
vantageous offers to return. It is easy to
understand how Gonzaga and those about him
missed the genial intellectual artist, the accomplished companion, the fascinating man of the
world. Happily for Belgium and Antwerp, and,
may we not add, happily for Rubens himself,
his native sovereigns, his old friends, Albert
and Isabella, had also that æsthetic sympathy,
which is a blessing to any bosom, and with it
a pride in the brilliant young Fleming. They
were bent on keeping him at home, for the
honor and profit of that home ; and, to attain
this end, they proceeded most judiciously.
They invited him to Court, and when he came,
they treated him with such distinction, and at
the same time with so much personal interest,
that Rubens could not but be gratified and **im-**
pressed. They at once engaged him to paint
their portraits, and appointed him official
painter, with a salary of five hundred gold
florins. The ministers, nobles, and other notable personages seconded the Archduke and
Duchess, and showered upon him kind atten-

tions. **Without hesitation** Albert granted his request, that **he** be permitted to reside in quiet Antwerp instead of in Brussels ; and Rubens established himself in the native city **of his** father and mother and of his forefathers. In his moments of highest triumph, of warmest inspiration, of intensest consciousness, what choice tears must have started from his eyes at the thought of that dear mother, and that she was not there to share with him his best. Had she been alive, the blandishments and favors of Royalty would not have been needed to refasten **him to his early home.**

It is not always easy for the shrewdest connoisseur **to** date the pictures of Rubens. With his exuberance of life and his fertility, he seems to have leaped early into possession of himself, as Keats and Shelley did, on entering manhood. It is, however, well known that one of the first works he executed after his return from Italy was a *Holy Family* for the Archduke Albert. This drew such admiration, that a **society in** Brussels, called that of St. Ildefonso, **at the** head of which was the Archduke, **and of which** Rubens himself had just been made **a member,** ordered from him an altarpiece for the Chapel **of the** order of St. James. "This picture," says

Waagen, "which is at present in the Imperial gallery at Vienna, represents the Virgin Mary enthroned, and putting the cloak of the order on the shoulders of St. Ildefonso. She is surrounded by four female saints. On the interior of the wings, are the portraits of Albert and Isabella, with their patron saints. This work, one of the most admirable ever painted by Rubens, displays in a remarkable degree the qualities praised in the one painted for the Archduke." The members of St. Ildefonso were so satisfied and delighted with their altarpiece that they sent him a large purse of gold. This Rubens, thanking them warmly, declined, saying that his only desire was to be useful to his brother members ; hereby showing at the same time the address of the man of the world and the refinement of the gentleman.

At that time, just after his eight years assiduous study of the great Italian masters, Rubens may be supposed to have been saturated with their juice ; but so deep was the spring and so rapid the flow of his native powers, that these pictures have the clear clean stamp of individuality. While, by a rich Italian experience, his fine faculties had been cultivated, perfected in their nimbleness, the marks of his culture were only visible in the superior command over his own resources. There is no borrowing from Michelangelo or Titian or any other. Easier, much easier, is it for a healthy, abundant man of genius to paint, or to write, out of his own inward fulness than to imitate another. Rubens had soul and strength and originality to have his own style.

To give him congenial employment was the best way to wean him from Italian yearnings. Brush in hand before a large canvas, was so much like being in Italy, that he could grow reconciled to his northern latitude ; and in the sympathy and the considerate kindness of the Archduke and Isabella he could feel that he had almost an equivalent for the munificent Gonzaga of Mantua. In addition to such employment, of which he was sure soon to have his hands full, he was about to bind himself to his native land by ties which, while planting him in Antwerp as a permanent dweller, were to bring to him in heaping measure the joys of domestic life. On the thirteenth of October, 1609, he was united in marriage, in the abbey church of St. Michael, to Isabel Brandt, the daughter of a magistrate of Antwerp and sister to his brother Philip's wife. For several years,

until his own house should be **ready, he** resided
with his father-in-law.

On what authority, of tradition or of more
trustworthy stamp, does M. Michiels call Isabel
Brandt *une Flamande assez lourde*, a heavy
Flemish woman? In the biographies she is
spoken of as beautiful (artists are apt to choose
such), and is so represented in the family-
group, painted by her husband for the family
chapel in the church of St. James at Antwerp.
A stereotyped, but much exaggerated, reproach
against Rubens is, that in historical and sacred
subjects, he takes for models of female figures
his heavy muscular countrywomen. As if the
female sex attained in Flanders to stouter,
coarser stature than in Germany or England.
Not only is this not the case, but in the upper
classes, — to judge by the nineteenth century,
— the female figure does not in Flanders tend
so much to overabundant *embonpoint* as in
England. Nor is there so frequent an exhibition of what in England and America **we** call
vulgarity, a quality in his women with which
Rubens has also been twitted.

Shortly after his marriage Rubens bought a
house, with spacious ground and garden, in the
street which now bears his name. He pulled

6

down the building, as wanting in two of the requisites of a dwelling for him, a roomy, easily accessible studio, and a hall or gallery for the rich collection he had brought from Italy. The father of Rubens, being the only child of a prosperous father, was a man of wealth. At the death, in 1608, of his widow, Marie Pypelincx, only three of their numerous flock survived. Peter Paul was thus heir to what might be called an independent fortune ; not, however, such as to justify the mansion he was about to erect. But in Italy he had been paid generous prices in cash and costly presents, and thus was enabled to gather treasures of art to send home ; and, moreover, he felt that he had a mine in his fingers. One day an alchemist, — one of those plausible pretenders, such as later levied large sums upon the more credulous Van Dyck, — applied to Rubens to tempt him to share the enormous profits about to be reaped from the discovery of the philosopher's stone. "I have discovered it myself," said Rubens. "Discovered the philosopher's stone !" exclaimed the man. "Yes," rejoined Rubens ; "come with me and I will show it to you." He led the gaping alchemist into his studio, and held up his pallet.

To most people, about to build a house for themselves to live in, the Latin saying, *parva domus magna quies*, a small house, large ease, were a pertinent reminder. But men and workers there are who must have space, — width, length and height for the gainful swing of their powers. Poems and philosophies may be, and have been, written in stunted attics ; but when the poet needs a canvas and frame ten feet square whereon to write his poem, space and broad approaches become necessities. Still more room was asked for the rare manifold handiwork of other and various artists which Rubens was so fortunate and foreseeing as to possess. Then, in the man himself there was a roominess and largeness that needed scope to expand in. And so Rubens built a palatial abode, a novel feature of which, after the manner of the palaces of Italian nobles, was a separate compartment for works of art. This he placed beyond the court-yard in form of a capacious Rotunda, lighted, like the Pantheon, from the top. Here he deposited and arranged the treasures collected in Italy, — pictures, marbles, vases of agate and porphyry, engravings, medals, cameos, gems, intaglios. Beyond the Rotunda was a large garden, planted with choice trees and shrubs and flowers.

One has a grateful satisfaction in thinking that Rubens was the possessor of these — luxuries shall we say? Call them, rather, refined utilities. Follow him from his studio, where, for two or three hours, his brain and hand have, by some high, particularly congenial theme, been strained to their utmost, when, laying aside that magical pallet, he descends to the Rotunda, there to unbrace and refresh his tasked faculties by communion with his loved colleagues of Italy and ancient Greece. Thence, for still subtler contacts, he passes into the garden, and there, under a sunny sky, amid leafy shadows and tender shrubbery, stooping now and then to caress an exquisite flower, he completes the refreshment. The poet-artist, in the presence of Nature's wonders, feels a rapture so gentle, that it soothes and rests his strong faculties while re-invigorating them.

VII.

THE DESCENT FROM THE CROSS.

A SIDE wall of the new house was found to have encroached on a neighbor, that neighbor being the guild of the gunsmiths, from whom the property had been purchased. Neither party being disposed to give way, a lawsuit was threatened, when a former burgomaster, and the foremost lawyer of the city, Nicholas Rockox, the president of the gunsmiths, who was also a personal friend of Rubens, assured him he would be beaten. A compromise was then agreed upon : the strip of land to be retained by Rubens, who, in exchange, was to paint for the gunsmiths a triptych, that is, a picture in three parts, a centre and two of half size, one on either of the folding shutters, the whole to be typical of the patron saint of the gunsmiths, St. Christopher. Rubens painted for them the *Descent from the Cross*, the name Christopher meaning in Greek, bearer of Christ. When finished, the picture was carried to the chapel of the gunsmiths in the Cathedral. The land, however (probably a thin strip), was not set off as an equivalent for the picture, Rubens, says M. Gachet, — who has published the original minutes of the transaction, — having received, from first to last, nine thousand francs, about eighteen hundred dollars, from the guild of the gunsmiths. It now hangs in the south end of the transept of the Cathedral, the corresponding place in the north end being filled by the *Elevation of the Cross*, a work which by some connoisseurs is esteemed equal to the *Descent*.

Although excellence of execution is the first requirement in any picture or poem, whatever the subject, yet, to choose well his subject is a deep part of the poet's gift. The genius of choice is more favorably exhibited in the *Descent* than in the *Elevation*. In the *Descent* the tragedy is there in all its grandeur and significance, but the agony is over: in the *Elevation*, the agony fills the eye and overfills the heart. Nought but the solitary sublimity of the subject, with the depth and universality of its interest to Christendom, justify the exhibition by art of such bodily suffering. Our sympathy is strained, and too much pained, which it is not in the *Descent*. Having, in another volume,[1] referred to this picture, I extract the brief paragraph.

"The spiritual and corporeal grandeur of this magnificent work, the strength combined with grace in the figures and in the grouping of them, the strain without distortion in the efforts and limbs of the principal agents in lowering the body, the pathetic tenderness with which they handle and receive the body, all of them proclaiming by look and posture and gesture how holy they regard it, the dignity and majesty stamped upon the compact group, the repose in the midst of action, the balanced splendor of the coloring, and, irradiating and giving to the whole its great power, the lofty life wherewith the whole and all the parts are instinct, as it were from within, — these rare and varied and combined excellences carry into the mind an impression so full and elevating and enduring as to justify the judgment of many, that this is among pictures the masterpiece of the world."

A very acute, and at the same time, broad and genial French critic, Gustave Planche, says of it,[2] "This work is, without doubt, one of the

[1] *First Years in Europe :* Boston, 1866.
[2] *Études sur les Arts :* Paris, 1855.

most important and one of the most admirable
which Rubens has produced.   To make use of
a phrase familiar to Italian writers, *The Descent
from the Cross* is in itself a school of painting.
If it does not contain the whole of his genius,
it shows us the best part of it ; had he produced but this one work, he would take his
place among the great masters of his art.   The
composition is full of grandeur and simplicity.
. . . . It must be acknowledged that, in this
work, Rubens has placed himself by the side
of the highest painters.   Whatever be our
preference, be our sympathy at Florence or at
Rome, at Venice, at Parma, or at Milan, we are
dazzled by the boldness of the attitudes, by the
profound knowledge which shines forth from
every part of this picture. . . . . Among the
nine figures which make up the picture, not
one but is to be commended for truth : movement of the body, expression of the heads,
everything is conceived with judgment, executed with fidelity."

M. Planche then proceeds to compare with
the *Descent* the *Crucifixion of St. Peter.*   With
him we will for a moment break the chrono-
logical line to speak of this, supposed to be the
last large work that Rubens executed, one uni-

versally regarded as among his very best, and
one at which he wrought with peculiar zeal, on
account of his affectionate memories of Cologne, and his love for the subject. It was
ordered for the church of St. Peter in Cologne,
by M. Jabach, a noted connoisseur of that city.
" All the parts of this picture," says M. Planche,
" are treated with a scrupulous care, with an
exactness, a precision, which astonish his warmest admirers. Without wishing to place the
Crucifixion of St. Peter above the *Descent from
the Cross*, I think that one must have seen the
first of these works in order to fully appreciate
the skill and knowledge of this powerful master. To consider only the invention, he has
produced many works of the same order ; but
if we speak of the execution, the most of his
works, compared with the *Crucifixion of St.
Peter*, will seem unfinished. Purity of con-
tours, delicacy of modeling, suitableness of
movement, all are united in this admirable
composition."

In his letter to Geldorp in London, through
whom the picture had been ordered by Jabach,
Rubens says : " If, however, I could choose
a subject after my own taste, relating to St.
Peter, I should take his crucifixion with his

head down. It seems to me there is in it for me that out of which I could make something extraordinary." St. Peter in the act of being crucified with his head down, his limbs writhing with pain, his half-open mouth uttering a groan of anguish, with six executioners busied about him !

Some of the best actors are fond of exhibiting on the stage the agony of death. With deference to them and to Rubens, we ask, are such pictures on the stage or on canvas very high art? The Greeks, it seems to us, had a much higher æsthetic perception, when they veiled, by some opportune means, a countenance distorted by suffering, mental or bodily.

The *Descent from the Cross* was painted in 1612 ; the *Crucifixion of St. Peter* in 1638. This interval of twenty-six years, how crowded with high performance ! Hundred after hundred of finished canvases, large and small, went forth to far and near from that central studio. Rubens had an almost unprecedented power of continuous work. When he finished the *Descent*, he had, it may be said, taken full possession of himself, of his inborn genius and talents, cultivated with most industrious and intelligent perseverance for almost a quarter of a century. In his thirty-fifth year, a master of the first class in his glorious calling, he had attained to what Goethe calls "the last achievement of Art, ease and lightness."

Rubens had too many admiring looks turned towards him to escape those of envy,—a sting which, on darting out to strike others, recoils to poison our own hearts. One of his rivals, who before his coming had held sway in Antwerp, invited him to a direct trial: each should paint a picture on a chosen subject, and umpires decide which of the two were the better. Rubens declined the challenge. He answered: " My attempts have been subjected to the scrutiny of connoisseurs in Italy and Spain. They are to be found in public collections and private galleries in those countries: gentlemen are at liberty to place their works beside them, in order that the comparison be made." Rubens was too sound in heart to feel envious of any one, and strong enough not to be troubled by the envy and jealousy of others. " Do well," he would say, "and people will be jealous of you: do better, and you confound them."

Besides his own well-doing, Rubens was teaching others to do well, training pupils who were only second to himself. They repaid him

with their work, filling up in his style, under
his eye, the outlines he drew. Orders for large
canvases came so fast for many years, that,
without congenial help, one hand could not
have met the half of them.

In the works of Rubens the most conspicuous
exhibition of his inexhaustible resources, of the
immensity and variousness of his imaginative
range, is in the invention and grouping. One
is astounded at such command and fertility, at
such prodigality of pictorial material. Hence,
while a chief attraction of his paintings is from
their glow of color, he shows well in engravings,
so much life, movement, dramatic power, is there
in all his handiwork. Some of the most skillful engravers of that day were trained by him
under his own eye. Now, whatever of the execution he put upon his able pupils, this funda-
mental, controlling element of invention was
always his own. He conceived, composed,
grouped each picture, and then with his own
hand drew the outlines.

He had been asked to paint for the Cathedral of Malines a picture of the Last Supper.
The canon who negotiated with him gave up
part of his own apartment, wherein to execute
the order, so that there should be no transpor-

tation with its risks. Rubens, when he had finished the drawing, sent one of his pupils, Juste
van Egmont (afterwards noted in France), to
lay on the ground-color. This was the greeting
van Egmont received from the canon : " Why
did your master not come himself ?" — " Don't
be uneasy," answered the young man, " he will,
as is his custom, finish the picture." Egmont
set himself vigorously to work ; the picture advanced rapidly, but no Rubens made his appearance. The canon worked himself into such a
rage, that he ordered the pupil to leave off work.
He then wrote to Rubens : " 'Twas a picture
by your hand I ordered, not an attempt by an
apprentice. Come then and handle the brush
yourself ; or recall your Juste van Egmont, and
tell him to take with him his sketch ; my intention being not to accept it, you can keep it for
yourself." Rubens answered him that he had
not been the victim of a fraud : " I proceed always in this way ; after having made the drawing, I let my pupils begin the picture, finish even
according to my principles ; then I retouch it
and give it my stamp. I shall go to Malines in
a few days ; your dissatisfaction will cease."

At so early a period after his return from
Italy, as when he painted the *Descent from the*

Cross, Rubens had hardly had time to train adept pupils. That and many others were wholly by his hand.

From a list and description of pictures offered to Sir Dudley Carlton, and from letters growing out of the negotiation, it appears that Rubens made a marked difference in price between those in which his pupils had had a share and those entirely by himself. Sir Dudley Carlton came to the Hague as ambassador from England in 1616. Soon after his arrival he made a short tour of travel, when, being in Antwerp, and a noted connoisseur, he of course saw Rubens. Among the letters relating to Rubens, published in 1859, by W. Noël Sainsbury, from papers preserved in the State Paper Office in London,[1] one of the first is from Tobie Matthew, an agent of Carlton, dated a few days after Sir Dudley's visit to Antwerp, and giving account of negotiations with Rubens for a hunting-piece. Matthew was authorized to give in payment a gold chain of Lady Carlton's. Rubens, however, required that the value of the chain be first ascertained from a goldsmith. In another negotiation, later, Matthew says:

[1] *Original unpublished Papers, illustrative of the Life of Sir Peter Paul Rubens :* London.

" The demands of Rubens are like the laws of the Medes and Persians, which may not be altered," calling him, in the same letter, because of his inflexibility as to price, " the cruell, courteous Paynter."

In the autumn of 1617, Rubens received a message in regard to some antique marbles which Sir Dudley owned, and was willing to exchange for pictures by Rubens. On the 17th of March, 1618, Rubens, after saying that, from pressure of business, he cannot come to see them, adds : " I, as being fond of antiques, would readily be disposed to accept any reasonable offer, should Your Excellency continue in the same mind ; but I cannot fancy a better expedient to arrive at some negotiation than by means of the bearer of this letter, to whom Your Excellency, being willing to show your collection, and permitting him to take an inventory, so that he may be able to give me an account of it, I will also send you a list of those works that I have at home ; or, should they be done on purpose, such pictures as would be more to Your Excellency's taste. In short, one could begin to form some negotiation that would be well for both parties."

The letters of Rubens are written in Italian,

and are translated for Mr. Sainsbury's volume.
The second one, dated Antwerp, April 28,
1618, we give entire, so characteristic is it of
the writer. Sir Dudley, in the beginning of
his letters calls his correspondent, " My very
illustrious and most kind sir."

" ANTWERP, *April* 28, 1618.

"MOST EXCELLENT SIR, — By the advice
of my agent I have learnt that Y. E. is much
inclined to make some bargain with me about
your antiques; and it has made me hope well
of this business, to see that you go earnestly
about it, having named to him the exact price
that they cost you: in regard to this I wish
only to confide in your knightly word. I am
also willing to believe you purchased them with
perfect judgment and prudence; although persons of distinction are wont usually, in buying
and selling, to have some disadvantage, because
many persons are willing to calculate the price
of the goods by the rank of the purchaser, to
which manner of proceeding I am most averse.
Y. E. may be well assured I shall put prices on
my pictures, such as I should do were I treat-
ing for their sale in ready money; and in this
I beg you will be pleased to confide in the

word of an honest man. I have at present in
my house the very flower of my pictorial stock,
particularly some pictures which I have retained for my own enjoyment; nay, I have
some repurchased for more than I had sold
them to others; but the whole shall be at the
service of Your Excellency, because brief negotiations please me; each party giving and receiving his property at once; and, to speak the
truth, I am so overwhelmed with works and
commissions, both public and private, that for
some years I can not dispose of myself: nevertheless, in case we shall agree, as I anticipate,
I will not fail to finish as soon as possible all
those pictures that are not yet entirely completed, though named in the herein annexed
list, and those that are finished I would send
immediately to Your Excellency. In short, if
Y. E. will make up your mind to place the
same reliance on me that I do yon ou, the
thing is done. I am content to give Your Excellency, of the pictures by my hand, enumer-
ated below, to the value of six thousand florins,
of the price current in ready money, for the
whole of those antiques that are in Y. E.'s
house, of which I have not seen the list, nor do
I even know the number, but in everything I

7

trust your word. Those pictures which are finished I will consign immediately to Y. E., and for the others that remain in my hand to finish, I will name good security to Y. E., and will finish them as soon as possible. Meanwhile I submit myself to whatever Y. E. shall conclude with Mr. Francis Pieterssen, my agent, and will await your determination, with recommending myself in all sincerity to the good graces of Y. E., and with reverence I kiss your hand.

"From Your Excellency's most affectionate Servant,   PETER PAUL RUBENS.

"To the most excellent, most esteemed, Sir Dudley Carlton, Ambassador of the Most serene King of Great Britain to the States of the United Provinces at the Hague.

"LIST OF PICTURES WHICH ARE IN MY HOUSE.

500 Florins.[1] 1. A Prometheus bound on Mount Caucasus, with an eagle which pecks his liver. Original, by my hand, and the eagle done by Snyders : 9 feet by 8.

600 Florins. 2. Daniel amidst many Lions, taken from the life. Original, the whole by my hand : 8 feet by 12.

[1] Gold florins, worth each about one dollar and seventy cents of our money.

600 Florins. 3. Leopards, taken from the life, with Satyrs and Nymphs. Original, by my hand, except a most beautiful landscape, done by the hand of a master, skillful in that department : 9 feet by 11.

500 Florins. 4. A Leda with swan and a cupid. Original by my hand : 7 feet by 10.

500 Florins. Crucifixion, large as life, esteemed perhaps the best thing I have ever done : 12 feet by 6.

1200 Florins. A Last Judgment, begun by one of my scholars, after one which I did in a much larger form for the most serene Prince of Neuberg, who paid me three thousand five hundred florins cash for it ; but this, not being finished, would be entirely retouched by my own hand, and by this means will pass as original : 13 feet by 9.

500 Florins. 5. St. Peter taking from the fish the money to pay the tribute, with other fishermen around ; taken from the life. Original by my hand : 7 feet by 8.

600 Florins. 6. A Hunt of men on horseback and lions, commenced by one of my pupils, after one that I made for His most Serene of Bavaria, but all retouched by my hand : 8 feet by 11.

50 Florins each. The twelve Apostles, with a Christ, done by my scholars, from originals by my own hand, which the Duke of Lerma has, each having to be retouched by me throughout: 4 feet by 3.

600 Florins. A picture of an Achilles clothed as a woman, done by the best of my scholars, and the whole retouched by my hand, a most brilliant picture, and full of many beautiful young girls: 9 feet by 10.

300 Florins. 8. A St. Sebastian, naked, by my hand : 7 feet by 4.

300 Florins. 9. A Susanna, done by one of my scholars, the whole, however, retouched by my hand : 7 feet by 5."

Sir Dudley would have none but pictures entirely by the hand of Rubens, and, in his answer to the letter with the list, says : "I do not dispute the prices, esteeming them reasonable, since they are not copies, nor the work of scholars, but all from your hand, just as the whole of the antiques show the hand of the master. . . . . You, Sir, may calculate on having in this collection of marbles the most costly and most precious *in hoc genere,* which no

Prince or private person, whoever he may be, on this side of the mountains can have."

As by rejection of those on which there had been any hand but the master's the value fell below that of the marbles, Sir Dudley proposes that the deficiency be made up by Brussels tapestry. Rubens, in answer, while not objecting to the offer of Sir Dudley, says : " Yet, Y. E. must not think that the others are mere copies, but so well retouched by my hand, that with difficulty they would be distinguished from originals, notwithstanding which they are put down at a much lower price : but I am unwilling to persuade Y. E. to this by fine words." Then, after a few lines, in which several words are lost from the Manuscript, he adds : " The reason I would treat more willingly in pictures is clear, because they do not exceed their just price in the list, nevertheless they cost me nothing, as every one is more prodigal of the fruits which they grow in their own garden, than of those that they buy in the market ; and I have expended this year some thousands of florins on my buildings, nor am I willing for a caprice to exceed the bounds of a good economist. In fact, I am not a Prince *sed qui manducat laborem manuum suarum.* I wish to in-

fer that if Y. E. wishes to have pictures to the
full amount, be they originals, or be they well
retouched copies (which show more for their
price) I would treat you liberally, and am always willing to refer the price to the arbitra-
tion of any intelligent person. If however you
resolve on having some tapestries, I am content to give you tapestries to your satisfaction
to the amount of two thousand florins and four
thousand florins in pictures."

Sir Dudley concludes one of his last letters
as follows : "And thus I have conformed in all
and every part to the contents of your last two
letters, save that I cannot subscribe to your
denial of being a Prince, because I esteem you
to be the Prince of Painters and of Gentlemen ;
and to that end I kiss your hands.

"From your most affectionate to serve you,

"DUDLEY CARLTON."

After several weeks of negotiation, in which
it would be hard to say which of the two had
shown the more courtesy and the more keen-
ness at a bargain, his Britannic Majesty's Ambassador or the "Prince of Painters," by the
end of May the barter was consummated by
interchange of the marbles and the pictures.

On the 1st of June, Rubens writes that he had
delivered the pictures, the whole in good condition, and packed with care: "In lieu of a
chamber furnished with marbles, Your Excellency receives pictures sufficient to adorn an
entire palace." Sir Dudley, through his agent,
must have requested Rubens to send him a
portrait of himself ; for, towards the end of the
letter occurs the following significant sentence :
" I shall most willingly send my portrait to
Your Excellency, provided you, reciprocating,
will be pleased to do me the honor to allow me
to have in my house a memorial of your person, conceiving it to be reasonable that I should
place a much higher value on you than you on
me."

At the end of this chapter is as fit a place
as will be found to insert a letter of Rubens
exhibiting the minuteness of his antiquarian
knowledge, of which he made use in his art
whenever occasion served. Pictures having a
value, a secondary value, as exponents of history, this correctness has its importance. In
further illustration of the attention Rubens
gave to historical detail, Mr. Sainsbury says :
" In several of his paintings of the Crucifixion,
and on his celebrated *Descent from the Cross*,

the scroll containing the superscription, written by Pilate, is not only written in real Hebrew characters, but .in the dialect of Aramæan or Chaldee used in Palestine at the time of the Crucifixion, that dialect which St. Paul most probably could read and write."

Two antiquarians, Mr. Swert and Mr. Camden, having a discussion about a statue of Isis, Swert gets the opinion of Rubens in a letter. In sending this to Camden, he calls Rubens "the antiquary and Apelles of our time." The letter of Rubens is in Latin, and was translated for Mr. Sainsbury's volume.

"ANTWERP, *Feb.* 1617–8.

"MY DEAR MR. SWERT, — To confess the truth, I have never been able clearly to perceive the Isis of our worthy friend Mr. Camden, nor indeed from a figure so rude (I ask the artist's pardon) have I been able to form a probable conjecture. As for the heifer, unless her existence be credited on the faith of Mr. Camden, I should say she were something else, as the shape, proportions, gait and pose wonderfully contradict the properties of an animal of her class. Apis, who is almost always represented on ancient marbles, at least as often

as I have observed, either by the side of Isis
or of Egypt himself, includes the proper
stature of an ox almost full grown ; his side,
furthermore, is symbolized by its peculiar mark
of a moon more than half full ; also, he has
the horns and other characteristics of an ox ;
but what girl has ever fondled a cow instead
of a lap dog, and has nursed it in her lap ?

"With regard to the garland and fillet very
usual in Isis, and indeed her inseparable accom-
paniment, they do not appear at all ; for, unless
I am deceived, no one ever saw her painted or
designed without a *sistrum*, which is her dis-
tinctive mark. But, lest I should say nothing,
although I would not venture to affirm anything for certain in a matter so obscure, *I will
observe,* — If this animal be an heifer, I should
suspect it to be for some vow for good harvests,
according to that verse, — Thou shalt make a
sacrifice for good harvests with an heifer ; this
being received as the interpretation, as the
patera (bowl) bearing corn would lead us to
suppose ; and the drinking vase in the other
hand, entirely different from the urns of rivers.
As the *laureæ* (laurel) crowns appropriated to
sacred rites were made of flowers, leaves, gold,
or any other material, as we may learn from

many examples. Good Sir, reckon this nothing
to the matter in hand, but for my affairs abun-
dantly sufficient, which call me hence away.
The inquiry concerning Isis, we must leave
entire and unaltered. Farewell, and continue
to love me always.

"Altogether yours,

"PETER PAUL RUBENS."

VIII.

RUBENS AND HIGH ART.

PLASTIC Art comes into being through the
power the human mind has to project out of
itself, in concrete forms of beauty, **its per-**
ceptions, thoughts, visions. We say *forms of
beauty*, because without illumination from the
beautiful, Art cannot see its way into existence ; wanting this spiritualizing light, the forms
are opaque, are shallow attempts to imitate nature. Art, genuine **Art,** is always an effort to
interpret nature, to give some glimpse of that
which is the soul of the apparent object or individual or combination ; and, in performing this
interpretative office, it addresses itself, not to **a**
mere superficial capacity in the beholder, **of**
perceiving outward shapes and likenesses, but
to the depths **in him,** aiming to reach these by
a presentation of somewhat of the inward, life-
giving essence, which essence dwelling in, and
a part of, the divinely beautiful, constitutes the
very being of that which the artist wishes to
represent, and which he cannot represent unless

m* have in him some sympathy with this inward spirit of beauty, sympathy with that which gives to person, conjunction, fact or event, its quality, its character, its being.

Thus the high office of Art is, to interpret life, and the warmer and larger part of life being lived in the feelings, Art's field is there ; and as Art only emerges into being through sensibility to the beautiful, it seeks always the finer possibilities of life. Life in man and in nature being infinite in degree as well as in variety, the artist works in that part of the boundless field where his own individuality finds most congenial play. The sympathy — one of many — Rubens had with animal vigor, and with power in tense action, led him to delight in representing lions. Had he painted a fight between a cat and a dog as vividly as he did the combat of Hercules with a lion, the cat and dog fight would remain the inferior work, because the feelings involved are lower. So, through the whole range of the numberless productions of Rubens ; so, through the whole range of pictorial representation ; each work rises on the scale of Art according to the amount and *quality* of feeling each displays. No excellence of execution could lift a cat and dog fight into high Art. To compass the heights which **are within its reach, and** ought to be its **aim,** Art must concern itself with moods of life wherein the higher emotions play the chief part, whether as dominant, triumphant, or out-raged. In the latter case we have the pathetic, than which Art can hardly present a grander exemplification than **the** *Descent from the Cross* of Rubens. To be high, Art must **appeal to** what in us is aspiring, noble, innocent, disin-terested, to our purer sentiment, to that which **is** expansive, and loftily and exclusively human.

The human head and countenance being the **best and** the highest and the most beautiful that our eyes can behold, human features and their infinite expression offer the choicest range in Art's higher domain. In many of Rubens's works we find this cardinal subject treated with a force and expression and beauty, which **leave** nothing to desire. But what seems to me **the** very greatest exhibition of the might **of Art** that I ever beheld is the *Madonna* **of** *Santo Sisto* of Raphael, in Dresden. In the two heads of Mary and the child Jesus, there is a meaning, a depth, a beauty, a grandeur, a splen-dor, that are unspeakable. They exalt you as **you** gaze at them ; they uplift yourself and all

humanity. In those two heads is a light, to
have kindled which was needed a spark from
the divine source of creation.

To be high, Art does not need a large canvas, nor many figures, nor an imposing subject,
historical or sacred ; it needs a subject of healthy
feeling poetically treated, a good pictorial invention executed with manipulating mastery.
When the artist has power to animate a large
space, as Michelangelo does in the Sistine
Chapel, or Raphael in the *Transfiguration*, or
Leonardo in the *Cena*, or Rubens in the *Descent*
and the *Elevation*, Art reaches its highest ; but
it is high in a speaking, luminous portrait, where
the painter has seized the best of the original
and given it vividly, heightening it with subtle
faithfulness. It is high whenever the artist can
adequately express, that is poetically express,
and with technical skill, pure, primitive, significant feeling. Some of its finest exhibitions by
Rubens are seen in his more finished sketches.
I recall especially one, with three or four Cupids
and a car with flowers, so sparkling with life
and buoyancy and joyousness, and with light,
that the rosy boys looked self-illuminated. The
grandest, broadest, most prized effort could
hardly give one a stronger impression of crea-

tive power, so vivid were they, so tingling with body's blood, so joyous. Of similar effect is a picture by Rubens in the Dresden Gallery, *Neptune Stilling the Tempest.* "At the command of Neptune, standing in a shell borne on the waves by sea-horses with heads and necks above water, and followed by sea-nymphs, the angry winds are reluctantly retiring. What breadth and freshness of conception, expression, and coloring! One is nerved by looking at this picture. Those three prancing heads are a great creation. Rubens has here brought to view the original types of the horse-species, the progenitors of the whole equine race, such fire is there and strength, such a nervous dilation in those heads, darting lightnings from eye and nostril. This picture is a Homeric masterpiece."[1]

In fertility of ideas none of his great compeers surpasses Rubens. The wealth of a forceful, prodigal, well-stored, cultivated mind flowed into and fed active pictorial currents. Smith, in his noted catalogue *raisonné*, in eight volumes, of all known works of Art, has to devote one entire large volume to Rubens. In 1620, he went to Paris on the invitation of

[1] *Scenes and Thoughts in Europe.* Second series. Boston.

Marie dei Medici, who, at the suggestion of Baron de Vicq, ambassador of Albert and Isabella to France, wished him to paint a series of twenty-one large pictures illustrative of her career. On condition that he be allowed to fulfill the commission in his studio at Antwerp, he undertook it, and with the aid (never more helpful) of his numerous pupils, completed the whole in two and a half years, returning to Paris to finish there the two principal members of the series. In a letter of Rubens's we get an insight into the thorough way in which he worked. In one of the series there are three Sirens, and he writes to M. de Chenniévres to retain three young ladies. With his position, fame, and character, he probably had a wide command of such.

"To M. DE CHENNIÉVRES. — I beg of you to arrange for us that there may be retained for me, in the third week which follows this one, the two ladies Cassaïo, from the Rue du Vertbois, and also that little niece Louisa, for I reckon on making three studies of Sirens, and these three persons will be to me of great succor and infinite help ; much on account of the expression of their faces, but still more from their magnificent black hair, which I should have difficulty in finding elsewhere ; the same with their figures."

It should not be omitted, that after his first visit to Paris, Rubens, out of gratitude, delighted de Vicq by painting and sending to him as a present a Madonna, which Michiels says was a masterpiece. On the second visit to Paris, as further tokens of regard, he painted the portraits of the Baron and his wife.

In that age, all cultivated men had their minds, and often their mouths and their pens, filled with the ancient, particularly the Latin, classics. The flood from the waters of the revival of learning had not yet subsided, while modern classics were few, and had taken no hold of education. Grecian and Roman mythology were still a power, not only over educated thought, but, indirectly, over the ignorant masses, through the paganism inherited by, and incorporated into, the Church. Hence in the Arts, classical Allegory was resorted to for expressing virtues and influences by means of mythological figures, — a proceeding which does not help but hinders the beholder, whose mind is hereby subjected to a double, distracting action, being partly withdrawn from the fact before him to a far-fetched emblem of the fact.

8

Rubens resorted probably to Allegory, especially in the Medici series, to gain a field for
more complexity of movement and for more
gorgeous display of color ; he had, of course,
his weaknesses. The whole series is more ambitious than effective as Art ; and, as the doings
of Marie dei Medici were of no signal profit
either to contemporaries or to posterity, they
have little value as history. But even here,
where, if anywhere, there was the opportunity,
the great Flemish master is never theatrical,
such sincerity was there always in his work.

The chief profit that Rubens had of the
ancients was not from their myths or their
literature, but from their sculpture. It might
seem that the audacity of many of his postures
and expressions, the frequent want of temperance, of restraint, in conception, go to prove
that the principles of Greek Art had not become the familiars of Rubens's mind. But may
it not be affirmed that, without a keen and fruit-
ful insight into Greek Art and the works of
those who had learnt most from it, his best productions would lack somewhat of their finest
quality, and the *Descent from the Cross* that
union of grace and grandeur which distinguish
it ? A man of sensibility and versatility will

sometimes learn more from those whose practice is even the opposite of his, and learn con-
sciously as well as unconsciously. The artistic
individuality of Rubens was so pronounced, that
it asserted itself often in overleaping bounds.
This is palpably apparent, whereas the chasten-
ing effect on him of the best Greek procedure,
being deeper and subtler, is to be traced in
the interior work of his happier moods. There
is, moreover, a false and constrained classic.
Would not a broad free view of Greek sculptors reveal that they too, the best of them, gave
into genial audacities akin to some of those of
Rubens ? How thoroughly he valued Greek
sculpture is made evident in an essay he wrote
in Latin, wherein he says : " I. am convinced,
that to reach the highest degree of perfection
as a painter, it is necessary, not only to be
acquainted with the ancient statues, but we
must be inwardly imbued with a thorough com-
prehension of them." How large and positive
were his opinions of Greek painting is shown
in a letter to Hadrian Junius of August 1, 1637,
thanking Junius for having sent him his work
on the painting of the ancients. After lament-
ing, says Waagen, how insufficient and deceitful
the conceptions must be which we form through

mere written accounts of the ancient Greek
painters, he continues : " For who amongst us,
if he were to attempt in reality to represent a
celebrated work of Appelles or Timanthus, such
as Pliny describes them, but would produce
something absurd, or perfectly foreign to the
exalted greatness of the ancients ? Each one,
relying on his own powers, would produce some
wretched, crude, unfermented stuff, instead of
an exquisite old wine, uniting strength and mel-
lowness, outraging those great spirits whom I
endeavor reverently to follow, satisfied, however, to honor the marks of their footsteps,
instead of supposing, — I acknowledge it can-
didly, — that I can ever attain to their eminence
even in mere conception."

Mrs. Jamieson, a disciplined, competent critic
of Art, is an intelligent appreciator and warm
admirer of Rubens ; nevertheless, in one of her
valuable notes to the English translation of
Waagen, she passes a judgment on him which,
without accepting it in full, is worth reporting :
" It appears to me, the whole tendency of Rubens's mind and genius might be called *Roman,*
in contradistinction to *Greek ;* Roman in its
grandeur, its vastness ; in a sort of irregular
contempt for the more refined rules of Art, in

the tincture of sensuality and ferocity, depraving at times the finest productions of his pencil."

In looking through Smith's exhaustive catalogue, which gives the whole fruit of Rubens's fertility, one is amazed at the productiveness, the overflowing prodigality, of a single brain ; for, the invention is all his in every case, the creative, the mind work, the plan and purport, however much of the comparatively mechanical may have been often the handiwork of pupils trained by himself. In the beginning of Waagen's book on the life and genius of Rubens is a list of the pictures referred to in the course of the essay. The list comprises over a hundred pictures, — not a tenth, however, of the number in Smith's catalogue, — and being divided according to subjects, presents at one view the unexampled range of his pencil.

Waagen is a little too hard upon Rubens on account of his " love for scenes of a coarse and sensual character." As such subjects are a very small fraction of the whole of his works, especially in comparison with the number on sacred subjects, on historical and on mythological, is it just to say, — implying thereby a

special fondness, — that. Rubens had a love for
such? He had a love for all subjects that
illustrate the passions and activities of human
nature. He was not a puritan, to reject a subject because it presented the grosser, lower
side of life. In the fullness of his human en-
dowment, he, like Shakespeare, could bear
with, nay, sympathize with, weakness and excess. We quote from Waagen: " Old Silenus
naked, and in a state of complete drunkenness,
led by two females, presenting every characteristic of the grossest animal nature; in the fore-
ground, perhaps, a fat female faun, unconscious
from beastly drunkenness, whilst two little
fauns are hanging at her bosom, and intoxicat-
ing themselves with her milk." A drunken
man reeling in the street is a pitiable, offensive
and most unpictorial spectacle, a sight hateful
to Gods and men ; but old Silenus in his rubi-
cund, rotund nudity! Why he was one of the
demigods ! And the little fauns, getting drunk
on their mother's milk : with the movement
and spirit of Rubens in it, it is the very poetry
of drunkenness. There is no odor of bad
whiskey about it : it has a Burgundian bouquet.
Aye, and is there not a moral in it for these
times, for all times ? It takes a poet, and a

thoughtful poet, **to compose such** a picture.
To competent artists, subjects which require
the nude are on that account especially accept-
able and desirable ; for, to the capable painter,
nakedness is his opportunity.

Rubens, like every whole, well-rounded man,
had an enjoyable, renewing sense of the comic.
Of this, and **at the same** time of the breadth **of**
his humanity, **one of the** most notable exempli-
fications is the famous picture in the Louvre
called the *Kermess.* Rubens **was not merely**
a temperate liver, — having **soon discovered**
that only through temperance could **he** have
full command and fruition of his manifold gifts,
— but he avoided jovial and kill-time parties ;
yet, with **what** heartiness he could enter into
the joviality of others, **is** exhibited in this
lively, veracious representation of a *Kermess,*
or peasant festival in Flanders. In front of a
village inn **about** fourscore **persons of both**
sexes are depicted, intermingled in varieties of
groups, in the full swing of boisterous enjoyment, after a better meal than peasants are
used to ; singing, dancing, talking, shouting,
gamboling, love-making. A large serious dog
tries to get his share by prying into a pail half
filled with empty platters. An abounding

scene of rustic revelry, in the groups and individuals a character and expression which only
warm genius, animating rich intellectual resources, could give.

Had there happened to be in the Louvre, instead of at Munich a *Last Judgment* by Rubens,
one could in a few moments pass from pictorial
comedy to awefullest tragedy, both alike in their
unexampled resources of bodily movement. But
the contrast can be well seen in engravings,
which are the more satisfying, the more intellectual a picture is.

I suspect that Rubens painted animals to
give his mind a partial rest, after it had been
stretched to its utmost by some of his most
strenuous Biblical or historical endeavors. He
could thus refresh his faculties, because animals are much easier to paint than men, and
because, at the same time he delighted to paint
them. Bears, wolves, dogs, wild boars, horses,
crocodiles, hippopotamuses, lions, tigers, leopards, are honored by his brush, which gets to
be so intimate with them, that it shows them
in all their grace, flexibility and animal power.
His wolf-hunts and boar-hunts and lion-hunts
are the best in that kind. It is related that he
caused to be brought to his house a very fine

and powerful lion that he might study him in various attitudes. But what he had still greater delight in painting than animals was children. Here too, as with animals, and in a higher form, he had what a healthy, juicy mind like his revelled in, nature unsophisticated. It may have been in front of one of his canvases, glowing with the luminous rosiness of half a dozen of these happy soul-buds, that Guido exclaimed: " Does Rubens mix blood with his paint ? " The mobility of children, their naturalness, their unveiled life and innocence, humanity in its heavenly promise, laughing incarnations of hope, all appealed to his liveliest sympathies, as to his artistic preferences.

Besides the rural views involved in hunts or *caccias*, — as, with his love of Italian, he called them, — and in other subjects, Rubens painted of landscapes proper some that are celebrated. Like thousands of other frequenters of the Pitti Palace in Florence, I have often stood in especial admiration before a large one, a hay harvest. Having been much at courts, his willing eye had feasted on the pomp and magnificence of regal show, and this too, on appropriate occasions, he transferred to canvas. From a wide and minute observation in more

modest spheres, he drew subjects from social
life, what are called *tableaux de genre*, to be
executed with equal skill and expressiveness.
There never was a great painter who was not a
master of portrait ; and accordingly Rubens
has left many admirable portraits, of youths
and burgomasters, of fair women and philoso-
phers, of kings and nobles, the whole crowned
by the incomparable *Chapeau de Paille*, of
which Waagen says : " No picture justifies
more than this the appellation which Rubens
has obtained, of the painter of light.   No one
who has not beheld this masterpiece of painting can form any conception of the transparency
and brilliancy with which the local coloring in
the features and complexion, though under the
shadow of a broad-brimmed Spanish beaver
hat, are brought out and made to tell, while the
different parts are rounded and relieved with
the finest knowledge and use of reflected lights.
The expression of those youthful features
beaming with cheerfulness, is so full of life,
and has such a perfect charm, that one is inclined to believe the tradition, that Rubens fell
in love with the original (a young girl of the
Lunden family at Antwerp) whilst she was sitting to him."   To this passage Mrs. Jamieson

adds a note: " The picture, as a picture, is miraculous, all but life itself. The bosom, as is usual with Rubens, is the least successful in the management. Rubens, during his life, would never part with this picture. It is simply designated in his catalogue as, 'le portrait d'une demoiselle, les bras croisés.' After the death of his widow it passed into the possession of the Lunden family, whose heir, M. Van Havre, sold it in 1817, for sixty thousand francs to another descendant of the family, M. Stier d'Artselaer. At his death in 1822, it was sold by auction, and purchased by M. Niewenhuys for seventy-five thousand francs, and brought to England, where, after being offered in vain to George IV., it was bought by Sir Robert Peel for three thousand five hundred guineas."

But where the affluence of Rubens shows itself, as that of a colossal as well as a refined organization, is in what might be called, as much on account of the space they fill as for their grandeur of presentation, the heroic departments of Art, those, namely, where the theme is taken from classical Mythology, or from sacred or profane History. In each of these provinces he has left masterpieces. He joyed in a wide, roomy subject,— his mind was so roomy,— subjects full of motion and expression. Justly has Rubens been called the painter of light ; he fills his pictures with light. There is light in the atmosphere around the figures, and light in the figures themselves. Than this illuminating gift there is none higher in the artist. Owing to this, his pictures are all cheerful, artistically cheerful, whatever the subject. Rubens has no black shadows ; his shadows are all penetrated by light ; hence, at times, their depth. In his pictures there is distance and freedom, and what perspective! and especially is there life, — life, which is the very condition of excellence in Art, as indeed in nature, excellence being in proportion to intensity of life.

In power there is magic. A large, rich nature, radiant with fruitfulness, imparts to whatever it handles an attraction which no one can resist ; and this it does out of the breadth and depth and excess of life in itself. Hence, there is a charm in any work of Rubens, even when the least poetical.

Was Rubens a religious artist ? Some critics call him a pagan. Michiels speaks of his "*fougue panthéistique.*" Rubens painted biblical and ecclesiastical subjects just as Leonardo and Titian and Michelangelo and Raphael

painted them, — because there was a demand
for such, — churches and convents being, in
those days, not only the chief buyers, but re-
quiring large canvases, just those which give a
great artist his best opportunity. In the fifteenth and sixteenth centuries the Catholic
Church wanted pictures as helps to worship.
Rubens and his fellows treated traditions of
saints and biblical subjects historically. In the
words of Ruskin, " they employed religious facts
for the display of Art." Rubens and Raphael
are not religious painters in the sense that Fra
Angelico is, of whom Mrs. Jamieson says : " In
the heads of his young angels, in the purity and
beatitude of his female saints, he has never
been excelled." Fra Angelico is nothing but a
religious painter ; and as religion is but a part
of humanity, he is a partial painter. Had Leonardo and Michelangelo and Raphael been like
him, born saints, there would have been no broad
bloom of Art in the sixteenth century. For its
unfoldment Art has need of all humanity, not
merely one side of it, just as Humanity, for its
unfoldment, needs all its higher powers and
aptitudes.

Religion, genuine religion, is the keystone of
the human arch ; but that this stone be a key,

there must be the arch. The keystone completes and binds the arch, and without it the
arch cannot be completed ; but without the arch
there is nothing to bind. The Greeks were a
very religious people, appealing to, relying upon,
their Gods. Yet their religion did not, could
not, save them from self-destruction through
selfishness and sensuality. Of the three chief
spiritual agencies to unfold, control, and uplift
humanity, — Do Justly, Love Mercy, and Walk
Humbly before thy God, — they had but one,
and that one performing but partially its function ; for you will not even walk humbly unless
you do justly and love mercy, as we may see
every day around us. The Greeks tried to
make their religion do the work of morality
and failed, just as the Jews failed, who did anything but walk humbly before their God, being
outswollen to the extreme of spiritual pride by
an intense egoism, whose self-flattering imagina-
tions were taken for religious inspiration. The
Roman Catholic Church, which inherited from
both Jews and Greeks, has in vain attempted
the same one-sidedness, which, like other one-
sidednesses, has a partial success, but cannot
of itself unfold and uplift humanity. Morality,
or the supremacy in conduct of all our spiritual

powers combined, is the human arch, wanting which the keystone religion cannot bind humanity. This supremacy is awaiting its consummation in a broader social order, when the interdependence of men shall be purer and deeper, and life on earth become more human and more heavenly.

IX.

THE DIPLOMATIST.

THE marriage of Rubens fell in the same year (1609) with the beginning of the truce between Spain and Holland. The long-banished quiet of peaceful years shed its productive calm upon the opening of his happy, glorious career in Antwerp. As the term of the truce drew near, negotiations were actively resumed, in the hope, especially on the part of Rubens, of ripening the truce into a permanent peace. Notwithstanding the cessation of hostilities for twelve years, the belligerents had by no means recovered from the devastation and exhaustion of forty years of war. Let this picture of Antwerp stand for the most of Belgium; it is from a letter dated at the Hague, Sept. 10, 1616 (the seventh year of the truce, therefore), and written by Sir Dudley Carlton : "untill we came to Antwerp, which, I must confess, exceeds any town I ever saw anywhere else, for the beauty and uniformity of buildings, height and largeness of streets, strength and fairness

of the ramparts. We stayed there (as in all
other places) one night only, having an afternoon and a morning to see the town, which we
performed in friends' coaches, whereby to give
our own rest, and left nothing of moment un-
seen. But I must tell you the state of this
town in a word, so as you take it literally,
magna civitas, magna solitudo, for, in the whole
time we spent there, I could never set my eyes
in the whole length of a street upon forty persons at once ; I never met coach nor saw man
on horseback ; none of our company (though
both were working days) saw one pennyworth
of ware either in shops or in streets bought or
sold." A few years later, towards the end of
the truce, Rubens himself writes of the pe-
cuniary depletion of all the Courts, adding, "as
for us, we have pawned our very shirts." Proof
it is of the tribute paid to Art in that age, and
of the renown of Rubens, that he had as much
as he could do, with the aid of numerous pupils.
Orders came mostly from abroad, and in the
latter portion of his career he had to decline
many.

The Archduke Albert esteemed highly the
judgment and trustworthiness of Rubens as a
statesman, so highly, that at his death in 1621

he commended him to Isabella as the man to
consult and rely upon in difficulties.

The war had been resumed languidly, and
efforts were making to bring about a peace between England and Spain as well as between
Holland and Belgium, when, in the midst of
his diplomatic activity, Rubens had to bear a
grievous loss in the death of his wife, after a
happy union of seventeen years. To a correspondent in Paris, M. Dupuy, who had written
to condole with him, he sends, on the 15th of
July, 1626, a letter of which this is the opening: " You are right in reminding me of the
inexorableness of fate, which does not bend to
the caprices of our passions, and which, as a
result of the supreme will, has not to account
to us for its decrees. It is for it to give orders
as absolute master; it is for us to obey, and
we have nought else to do, in my opinion, but
to make this servitude as little hard and as honorable as possible, by submitting to it willingly.
At this moment that I am writing, it is a duty
which seems to me very heavy and very insup-
portable. For this you recommend me to rely
upon time, which, I hope, will do for me that
which reason should do; for I have not the
pretension of ever reaching a stoical passivity,

nor do I believe that feelings so well in accord with their object ought to be suppressed, nor that all things in this world are equally indiffer ent, *sed aliqua esse quæ potius sint extra vitia quam cum virtutibus*, and that certain things carry with them feelings *citra reprehensionem*. I have, indeed, lost an excellent companion, who could easily be loved, nay, who could not but be loved, for she had none of the faults of her sex; without feminine humors or weak-nesses, but all goodness and modesty; for her virtues beloved by all while she lived, and since her death universally mourned."

The remains of his wife were placed in the same tomb with those of his mother and of his brother Philip, in the church of the Abbey St. Michael, and over them Rubens erected a monu-ment with an inscription.

Immediately after this he made a short tour into Holland, either secretly commissioned by Isabella, or simply to get some distraction in his sorrow. When at Rome, he had known, and formed a friendship with, Poelenberg of Utrecht, a noted painter on ivory. To him he wrote, announcing the death of his wife and his intended visit to Utrecht. At the first town where he stopped, Gouda, he fell in with

Sandrart, a brother-artist from Germany, who was rejoiced to meet the renowned Fleming, and offered himself as *cicerone* in the tour. At Utrecht, Poelenberg received them with warmth. Another painter, of some name in his day, Gerard Honthorst, lived too in Utrecht. They found him at work on a Diogenes, who, lantern in hand, is searching the streets of Athens, in broad daylight, for an honest man. In honor of his distinguished visitor, Honthorst put in Rubens as the man searched for, and himself as Diogenes. Rubens purchased the picture, as he did a number from Poelenberg, Bloemaert, and other artists whom they visited on the journey. He delighted to add to his princely collection by purchase from contemporaries.. With the wealth earned by his uncommon genius, kept prolific by his uncommon industry, Rubens could purchase like a Prince; but his fellow-artists he always treated like brothers, and for what he bought of them he paid liberally, generously.

Previously to this short tour in Holland, Rubens as the principal adviser of Isabella, and the true friend of her and of Belgium, was the central and most active agent in negotiations which involved nearly all the nations of Europe.

Evidence of his activity in 1624 is recorded in
the official correspondence of the two French
envoys at Brussels and at the Hague. The one
at Brussels writes : " Rubens rides often from
Brussels over to the camp of the Marquis Spinola, and gives out that he has some secret
understanding with Prince Henry of Nassau."
Eight days later, the same envoy writes : " I have
discovered that Rubens, in these negotiations, is
actuated purely by selfish motives and the desire
to secure an inheritance which he expects from
an uncle of his wife, who holds an office in Holland." On the 16th of September of the same
year the colleague in the Hague writes : " I learn
that the painter Rubens is an emissary of the
Cardinal de la Cueva, not for the purpose of
bringing about a truce, but rather to hinder it,
through the inconsiderate zeal habitual to such
persons, in whom imagination is much stronger
than judgment." A precious pair of envoys !
the one so far-sighted as to see in Holland
a rich uncle-in-law, never visible to any but a
vision so sharp as his ; the other, making of
Rubens the catspaw of a Cardinal who cun-
ningly used the uncontrollable imagination of
the artist to bring about a result the opposite
of that which Rubens personally desired ! The

primary qualifications of a serviceable agent are, not to underrate your opponent, and to be able to see men and things as they are. How the shrewd, pitiless, catlike countenance of Richelieu must have wrinkled in scorn when he read such dispatches from his minions, — he who never deceived himself, however much of his business was to deceive other people.

The error of the French envoy at the Hague in regard to Rubens is not an uncommon error; rather is it a pretty general one, namely, that what are called men of imagination (of poetical imagination is meant) are wanting in mental solidity, in clearness of judgment. In the first place, no man can do any kind of work without imagination; for imagination is simply the power of forming images in the mind, of conceiving, of grasping with the intellect materials gathered by thought, just as physical materials are grasped by the hand. This capacity of forming images and holding them distinctly and tenaciously, is the first need for success in anything above mechanical routine. When there is thoughtful planning on a complicated scale, this imaginative power (which is simply the highest degree of intellectual action) must be strong and persistent; and when the planner enters a new field, devising new combinations, a still broader and finer exercise of the power is called for ; and when he thus plans and devises under the impulse of a longing for the better, of a yearning toward perfection, then his mind becomes poetical in its devices, that is, creative ; and this is the highest state the human mind can reach, its vision being then the clearest and farthest and deepest, peering into the core of men and things, perceiving their finest relations, having insights which no other mental condition can gain, and, in union with strong thinking faculties, attaining to the highest practically productive efficiency.

When Rubens painted, he worked with a quick, powerful intellect, and this intellect — under sway of feeling, especially feeling for the beautiful — he employed, first to plan and group inwardly in his mind, and then to embody outwardly ; apprehending the capabilities of his subject and the relations of its constituent figures more clearly than possibly can any unpoetic painter. When Rubens talked to his friend and sovereign, the Archduke Albert, on political relations, being a poetical man, that is, a man of creative mind, who had observed much, and

could not help thinking much, he uttered opinions reached through his creative insight, which
insight was a divine gift humanly cultivated ;
and thus he impressed Albert, as he did other
competent men, as being a statesman of a high
order, who could in that field discern the bearings of men and circumstances with exceptional
clearness. All sound statesmen have more or
less of this inward, partly unconscious, power.

In giving an account of what may be called
a diplomatic episode in the career of the great
Flemish painter, my aim of course is, to present, as effectively as may be, a picture of Rubens, his character and capacity, as exhibited
in this phase of his life's doings. Therefore,
from the voluminous diplomatic correspondence
are extracted only such portions as strictly serve
the above purpose. How important was the
part played by Rubens, and what the esteem
in which he was generally held, are shown, as
in other documents, in the following letter from
him to Gerbier. Balthazar Gerbier was master
of horse to the Duke of Buckingham. The
Italics are probably retained in Sainsbury's valuable volume from the manuscript in French.
This letter is in several respects so significant
that it is given in full.

" Antwerp, *May* 9-19, 1627.

" Sir, — Your silence astonishes me, and makes me doubt whether our packets were rightly addressed. In a correspondence of such importance, letters received should always be acknowledged, as in case of any mischance it might be remedied by duplicates. You will see by the inclosed, from the Ambassador of Savoy, that we have been together at Brussels, and I confess, on my part, to have received all the satisfaction in the world. The Ambassador of Savoy sends his compliments, with the Infanta, and Spinola. He would only enter into the matter (*mistère*) through my means, and having found him as well informed as ourselves, *it has been thought proper to treat with him in sincerity, and without any reserve or afterthought.* I have informed him by the express order of Spinola, very exactly, of the present state of the business, and most entirely assured him of the good and holy intentions on our side. Also I can inform you that we have had something on the part of 70 [Spain?] which gives us courage, and makes us hope well for the success of the business ; but it is not sufficient to put it in execution. We believe that by Divine grace the rest will soon follow. I have returned to Ant-

werp, having unravelled the business, and put
Scaglia [Ambassador from Savoy] and Spinola
so near to one another, that they can talk over
the business of the Treaty ; nevertheless, they
have always done me the honor in any doubt,
scruple, or ambiguity, on either side, to allow
me to clear it up.   I do not now think there is
any difficulty between them ; they understand,
and are very well satisfied with each other,
showing no distrust.   Indeed, we find Scaglia
extremely able in affairs of such importance,
and I am very glad he has formed the resolu-
tion of going to Holland, for all the debate will
be, as I have said to Scaglia and you *oftentimes
before, upon the pretension of the States to bear
the name which they have in effect now.*   Scaglia
told me that he thought you would come and
find him in that quarter.   I should esteem myself very happy to be able to meet you, but I
believe my Masters dare not send me of their
own accord, otherwise I am of opinion that my
presence would greatly serve in promoting the
business by clearing up, between ourselves,
the difficulties heretofore debated : *for having
been employed in this treaty continually since the
rupture, I have all the papers presented on both
sides in my hands.*   We could consult together

with Scaglia **and Carlton.** This is why I beg
you to find means that this requisition be made
to Buckingham, and to write me a letter to **this**
effect, saying that he sends you to that part in
charge of many things which could not be safely
or easily trusted to paper, and that he dares **not**
send you back again to Brussels on account of
the reports it would give rise **to,** as before ; **but**
notwithstanding his Excellency **wishes** that I
should go **there with the** permission **of** my
superiors, to meet you on the happy circum-
stance of Carlton and Scaglia being also there.
This would be a *grand coup,* for, as I have told
you, all difficulties which might hinder or at
least render this *fine chef-d'œuvre incomplete,*
consist in the business of the States. I have
friends there of high standing, and my old
correspondents, **who would** not **fail to do their**
duty. I pray you see that this **be done, but on**
condition of an inviolable faith **to keep this, my**
request, secret, without it ever being known that
it **was** made through my instruction. Scaglia
will be in this **city** the day after to-morrow, and
we have sent his letter for a passport from the
States. I am well satisfied they will be of my
opinion touching **my** going there, although I
have not broached this to him, intrusting the

secret of this letter with you only to communicate it to Buckingham ; but you must, by the
same means, at least by Carlton or Scaglia, immediately obtain by entreaty a passport for me.
I intreat you to answer this immediately ; also
as to the particulars already written so many
times touching the remainder of the paintings
belonging to Buckingham, which I dare not
send without your order, seeing the passage is
so embroiled and dangerous that I would not
venture to undertake it without your express
order.   And, having nothing else to say, I very
humbly kiss your hands, and commend myself
to your good favor, ever remaining, Sir,

  " Your most humble servant,

    " PETER PAUL RUBENS.

" I beg you to burn this letter so soon as you
have done with it, for it might ruin me with
my masters, although it contains no harm, it
would, at least, destroy my credit with them,
and render me useless for the future."

As further proof of the respect entertained
for Rubens, and of the confidence in him, the
Duke of Buckingham, immediately after the arrival of this letter, sent Gerbier to Holland to
coöperate with the British Ambassador, Sir

Dudley Carlton. **Rubens stood** well with all
parties, with the rulers **of Spain, of England,
of Holland.** They believed him to be earnest
and **honest,** and thought him very capable.
He lay under this disadvantage, that the wishes
of his mistress, Isabella, and those of her **mis-**
tress, Spain, were not harmonious. Isabella
warmly desired peace with Holland ; Spain,
darkly folded **in the** veil **of** Castilian **pride,**
could not, because she would not, see things
as they were, and, although impoverished and
utterly disabled, was still **averse to** yielding,
even to necessity. **Belgium** being but a vas-
sal of Spain, Rubens, even though backed by
Spinola **as** well **as** Isabella, could **not** be as
explicit **as he** wished to be, and drew upon him
the doubts of Carlton. Carlton was more ready
to descend to the level of the painter, and chaf-
fer on equal terms about statues and pictures,
than to lift the plebeian up to his **ambassa-**
dorial elevation, **to settle on equal terms the**
peace of Europe.

Three days before the date of his **letter** to
Gerbier, Rubens, in one to his **friend** Dupuy
in Paris, touching incidentally on public mat-
ters, thus writes : " **Here** secret relations are
kept up with **Holland ; but you** may be assured

that Spain has authorized no negotiation in any
form whatever, notwithstanding the dispositions
shown by our Princess and the Marquis Spinola
to further the public good, which depends on
peace."

Five months later, Gerbier writes to Lord
Conway, English Secretary for foreign affairs :
" Rubens in a little note tells me that he wishes
the fleet would soon fall in with ours, and the
Spaniards get a good drubbing, so that the im-
petuosity of the Count d'Olivares might be the
means of doing good in some way."

It was in 1625, and in Paris, that Rubens
made acquaintance with and captivated the
magnificent Duke of Buckingham, one of the
most spoiled of the children of fortune. In the
autumn of that year, on his way to negotiate
a treaty with Holland, Buckingham stopped in
Antwerp to see Rubens, and was struck with
wonder and admiration at his collection. This
was then probably the finest in the world ; for,
the foundations were hardly then laid of the
National Galleries which are now the most attractive treasures of London, Paris, Dresden,
and other capitals. By the offer of ten thousand pounds sterling, the Duke tempted Rubens to sell him the best part of the collec-

tion, on condition that plaster casts of the antique marbles, taken at the cost of the purchaser, be left in place of the originals. The price was at the time deemed enormous. The identical antiques and pictures (thirteen of them by Rubens himself) would doubtless bring to-day at auction much more than one hundred thousand pounds sterling.

Rubens being soon recognized by the various negotiators as the superior mind among them, and inspiring trust from his solidity of character and evident sincere desire for peace, — which, behind all their intrigues, the most of them secretly wished for,— he was for several years the recipient of confidential and semi-official communications. Through these he had knowledge of all the diplomatic threads of the period, their bearings and inter-crossings. Isabella, from frequent cordial conference with him, becoming aware of this, made it known to Spain. Olivarez immediately wrote to have these papers delivered to the Spanish government. To this Rubens replied, that some were in cypher and could only be interpreted by himself, and that many of the others would be equally unintelligible to a third party. Hereupon the Junta of· Spain, by a *consulta* of the fourth of June, 1628, recommended that Rubens be summoned to Madrid. This is the cause of the second visit of Rubens to Spain. He went, not as an official envoy of Isabella, but because he was sent for by the Spanish government to give information which, as diplomatic agent for Isabella during several years, he alone could give. Once in Madrid, face to face with king and ministers, they became impressed, as others had been, with his sagacity and uprightness.

Several years before this, the King of Spain had ennobled Rubens, " regard being had to the great renown which he has merited and acquired by excellence in the art of painting, and rare experience in the same, as also by the knowledge which he has of histories and languages, and other fine qualities and parts which he possesses, and which render him worthy of our royal favor, we have granted and do grant to the said Peter Paul Rubens and his children and posterity, male and female, the said title and degree of nobility, etc." In consequence of this, the Infanta Isabella made him " gentleman of her household," a post which no plebeian could obtain.

Rubens arrived in Spain toward the end of August, 1628. As one who was intimately versed in the diplomacy of the last few years, his coming was of high value to Olivarez. As the greatest painter of the age, most valuable was it and welcome to another Spaniard, just rising into renown, a renown which has strengthened with time: this was Velasquez. Velasquez was one to prize the privilege of talking with his great Flemish compeer and of seeing him work. They appreciated each the other. Velasquez could learn from Rubens, and Rubens from him; for, Rubens was one of that vigilant elastic order of minds that never grow too old to learn. They suited each other: they became intimate. Rubens was then fifty-one, Velasquez twenty-eight. To the young, aspiring Spanish artist new and wider horizons were opened. The influence of Rubens it was that sent Velasquez to Italy a few months after the departure of his valued friend.

While in Spain on this second visit Rubens painted many pictures, M. Villaamil says forty in the nine months; and here he had no pupils to help him. Saying this is not meant to praise rapidity as of itself a virtue.

Olivarez wanted to gain time; Rubens wanted never anything better than to paint picture after picture: and thus the postpone-

ment of his return suited them both. At last,
on the twenty-ninth of April he set out, em-
powered by Phillip IV. to make a treaty of
peace with England, and carrying a document
which gave to Isabella authority to establish at
once a truce with Holland. Here was a mission of importance, and here the man to perform it.

Rubens loved Flanders, as every sound-
hearted man loves the land of his birth and
abode. In him this healthy feeling of patriot-
ism was heightened by what he individually had
done for his country. To the love, as of a child
for its parent, he added some of that of the
parent for his child. To his country he had
given a larger, finer fame. Through him,
Flanders, Antwerp, had become, to all European ears, names of fuller, more musical meaning. And to-day, as the traveler approaches
Antwerp, the far-twinkling spire of the Cathedral (itself worth a voyage to behold) reminds
him that this is the home of Rubens, that here
he lived and loved and wrought, and that here
still are many of the resplendent products of
his puissant brain, the most precious possession
of the famous old city, — most famous through
him.

Just before his departure from Spain, the king appointed **Rubens** secretary to his Privy Council, a post of great honor.

Passing through Paris, Rubens arrived about the middle of May at Brussels, to the joy of Isabella, who, as a true friend to the country she ruled over, had always desired peace. Stopping but four days at his home in Antwerp, he hastened to Dunkirk to embark on an English ship, thereby avoiding all risk of capture by Dutch cruisers. Bearing on this embarkation, here is, from Charles I., a note, the first part of which is apparently of a playful character :—

KING CHARLES I. TO THE EARL OF HOLLAND.

" Holland :

" This is only to bid you tell Mr. de Ville that if he be not content to go in my ship to Dunkirk, although it should retard his journey some hours, that I will complain of him to Rosabella, for if he go not in my ship, Rubens's journey will either be hindered, or I shall lie open to almost a just exception to those that are no friends to this treaty. So going to sleep I rest

" Your loving, constant friend,
" CHARLES R."

The painter Rubens was serviceable to the diplomatist Rubens. His pallet was often a passport of familiar admission to presences where envoys were admitted ceremoniously and seldom. The accomplished, winning, commanding Cavalier, with brush in hand (the maulstick he did not use, his nerves were so steady), would charm and persuade and overcome a royal or noble adversary in the easy intercourse of painter and sitter. Charles I., much prepossessed in favor of the illustrious artist, gave him just the opportunity Rubens desired by sitting at once for his portrait.

In his valuable volume, *Rubens Diplomatico Español*, M. Villaamil publishes most of the letters written (chiefly in Italian) from London to Spain by Rubens. Some were missing from the Simancas archives, but enough are preserved to make the reader admire anew the capacity of the writer, and his complete competency for the high and difficult task he had undertaken ; while one wonders at his power of work. To his chief in Madrid, Rubens gives clear, minute descriptions of the men and their relations to one another, — ambassadors, diplomatic officials, members of parliament, ministers, — all who then in London had any bearing

upon the important object he was sent to compass. He enables Olivarez to see the position
of affairs, and the actors in them, as distinctly
as when he had a story to tell on canvas. Rubens entered upon the business intrusted to
him with the zeal of a true patriot, who bent his
whole, capable, vivid mind to relieving from the
multiform miseries of war his dear country,
which, for half a century, had been subjected
to the tyranny, arrogance, ambition, extortion
and persistent incompetency of the Spanish
government.

It was in London that a nobleman,—with
the superciliousness with which the artificially
elevated are apt to bear themselves towards
those whom nature has placed on high, and
with perhaps a smack of the envy which the
favorites of fortune often feel towards the children of light (and *vice versa*), said to Rubens;
" The ambassador amuses himself with painting occasionally." — " No," answered Rubens,
" the painter amuses himself with diplomacy."

M. Villaamil, who seems to have no undue
partiality for Rubens, pays him this tribute :
" Those of us who have been in the diplomatic
career, and from a post in a legation have done
our share in making known to our own country

what it wishes to know of all that took place in that where we happened to be, discover in the correspondence of Rubens what a consummate diplomatist he was, how much tact he had, how prudent, active, forbearing, and patient to the last degree, and, above all, throwing aside all personality, how exclusively careful he was neither to exceed nor fall short of the line laid down to him from Spain, softening, when it seemed harsh, what the Count-Duke [Olivarez] had charged him to communicate, and even taking on himself faults, and errors which he had not committed, when by such assumption he could advance his objects and gain the ends he had in view in the service of Spain."

While performing, minutely and efficiently, his diplomatic duties, Rubens found time to paint pictures. The first, — and one of his best, — he painted for Charles I. In the catalogue of the King's Gallery, it is called " A picture of Peace and Plenty, with many figures as big as life, by Rubens." This picture, as interesting from the time and occasion of its birth as it is precious for its excellence, after traveling to Italy to pass a century in the Balbi and Doria palaces in Genoa, returned to England, and was finally bought by the Marquis of Stafford for

£3000, and by him presented to the National Gallery ; assuredly on all accounts the fittest spot for its final resting-place. Mrs. Jamieson, to whom we are indebted for these facts, reports Irvine's (a picture dealer) description of it as containing "almost everything in which Rubens excelled, — women, children, a man in armor, a satyr, a tiger, fruit and furies."

While in London Rubens made sketches, nine in number, for the pictures, ordered by the King, to represent on the ceiling of the throne-room in Whitehall, the deeds of James I. These pictures, the figures of which were of colossal size, were finished later in Antwerp. The price paid for them was £3000.

As a crowning of the rewards and honors heaped upon Rubens in England, the King knighted him, and after the ceremony presented him with the sword with which it had been performed. On taking leave he received a handsome service of plate and rich chain of gold to which was attached a miniature likeness of the King ; this he ever after wore round his neck.

The diplomatic career of Rubens was not yet finished. In 1632 or 1633, Isabella, having increased confidence in her wise counsellor,

sent him to Holland on a special mission.
This gave umbrage to the chief noblemen of
Belgium, always jealous of the diplomatic employment and efficiency of Rubens, the usual
jealousy of the pretentious incompetent towards
the competent being embittered by the hatred
which the inheritors of titles and political position harbor towards those who have earned
them by personal merit. Isabella, whose relation to these titled magnates was just then am-
biguous, had to yield, and recall Rubens. The
old Duke of Arschot, ambassador of Isabella
to Holland, one of the most pretentious and
empty of these nobles, and who, moreover, as
Gerbier states, had a " great aversion to Rubens," took offense, first, that Rubens did not
deliver to him certain papers relating to the
negotiation which papers, it seems, Isabella had
forbidden him to give up, — and, secondly, that
when required to do so, instead of coming in
person to make explanations, he had written a
letter to the Duke. The Duke, in the madness
of his aversion and jealousy, deemed the act of
Rubens in writing to him an assumption of
equality with him and therefore an impertinence! The letter of Rubens was only too
modest and respectful. Hereupon d'Arschot

writes him an insulting note. This nominal leader, this *Duke*, took advantage of his factitious eminence to put an affront upon the real leader, and, from his pride of place treated his superior with indignity, being so ignorant and obtuse as not to be able to recognize him. To the cost of poor Belgium, d' Arschot and his colleagues had for generations proved, what all history proves, to-day as emphatically as in the past, that where intellect and character do not rule, there will be misrule. The honest time has not yet come when men will stand each on his veritable self, and have influence and acceptable government over others just in proportion to his superiority; but we are nearer to it than in the days of Rubens and d' Arschot.

It is something beggarly when a man without merit tries to make a great ancestor piece him out. A man who personally lacks worth should be ashamed, instead of proud, to boast of ancestry whose superior worth makes them historical. From such progenitors such a descendant has no right to borrow : he has nothing to pay back with. All that an out-at-the-elbows beggar has to do is to beg : he can't borrow. It is related of the present Duke of Wellington that after his father's death, the

first time that he had to sign a letter, he drew
back : he felt a diffidence, a shame, he, an un-
distinguished individual, to assume and write
as his own that great resounding name. As
for our dull d' Arschot, this insult to Rubens
turns out to be a kind of honor to him : it res-
cues from oblivion his name by linking it to
that of his illustrious countryman and contemporary.

As for Rubens, it was well for him to have
this mortification : he had not had his share of
the depressive, the disheartening. Even when
not needed for direct correction, such humiliations are medicinal : they help to clarify the
currents of a life, and to give them steadiness.
In a fine organization, if they are not supplied
from without, they spring up within from one's
own ideals and aspirings. Rubens had an inward regulative force. His was too well-poised,
too high-strung a nature, to be spoilt by worldly
success. There is no evidence that he pre-
sumed upon his prosperity and renown. There
are no anecdotes of arrogance or forwardness,
or intolerance, or pride of purse. For the latter most ignoble of human frailties he had too
much breadth of moral being, and manly self-
respect.

For such an indignity, which signalized the
conclusion of his diplomatic career, besides the
daily amends in honors, homage, renown, and
troops of friends, Rubens had in those years a
fresh source of happiness. Towards the close
of 1630, having been a widower since 1626, he
married, for his second wife, Helena Fourment,
a beautiful girl of sixteen, Rubens being fifty-
three. The disparity in years seems not to
have been a source of evil consequences.
Helena, besides sitting as model for her husband's choicest female figures, proved herself
a good and faithful wife, and bore to him five
children during the latter ten years of his
life.

By his first marriage Rubens had two chil-
bren, both sons, Albert and Nicholas, the elder
being godson to the Archduke Albert. Both
survived their father, and Albert inherited
from him his fondness for learning, but not his
æsthetic genius. It was of this son that Rubens wrote from Madrid to his friend and
nephew, the learned Gevaerts of Antwerp, on
the twenty-ninth of December, 1629: "I en-
treat you to place my little Albert as my Image,
not in your Oratory, nor in your Infirmary, but
in your Museum. I love that child, and I rec-

ommend him to you in a serious manner, to you the chief of my friends, the Priest of the Muses, to take the greatest care of him with my father-in-law, my brother-in-law Brandt, both while I live and after my death."

X.

An original man of genius, of a mould at once stout and graceful, full of life, vigor, spontaneousness, — what a gift to a community! Through Antwerp and Flanders shone a brighter, finer light, when the influence of Rubens began to be felt. Able to bring rapidly into being a fresh, numerous, active brood of pictorial offspring, he was a creator in Art, the founder and chief of a school. In this character he gave the strongest evidence of might, by hatching, through warmth and care, a full nest of artistic mates. If he did not create, he revealed genial capacity, which, but for him, would have lain dormant or been partially unfolded. Among contemporaries, immediate predecessors and followers, he towers above all, somewhat as Shakespeare does above his, but not so unapproachably ; for, no one rose so near to the height of Shakespeare, as Van Dyck to that of Rubens.

To be admitted into his studio as pupil was

a favor ; and, using his pupils for assistants, he doubtless accepted only those whom his practiced judgment assured him had unusual talents for Art.   Michiels[1] affirms that all the pupils of Rubens became famous ; Van Dyck, Jordaens, Snyders, Teniers, Gérard Seghers, Juste Van Egmont, Erasme Quellyn, van Thulden, Jean Van Hoeck.

Every one of these wanted something that Rubens had.   And, besides the greater completeness in equipment, there was in Rubens that strong inward continuous fermentation of power, that active plenitude of mental life, that soul-pulsation, which momently replenishes the faculties and keeps them electrified for their high function.   Each of his pupils could travel prosperously on the broad track he had opened, but not one of them had himself light to reveal to the vision new pathways.

The leader of this proficient band was Antony Van Dyck.   In larger measure than any of his companions Van Dyck had the decisive

---

[1] ALFRED MICHIELS : *Rubens et l'école d'Anvers.*   M. Michiels has taken much pains to get biographical facts in regard to the pupils of Rubens, and to rectify mistakes of previous writers.   Relying upon his knowledge as well as his fidelity, in preparing this chapter I draw largely from his valuable volume.

artistic gift, the poetical. Hence, in his work there is fresh life to-day ; for, the poetical or creative, — which gives sign of itself by the sparkle of beauty, — when seconded by the talents whose combination insures adequate execution, breathes into its products the principle which preserves them.

Van Dyck was twenty-two years younger than Rubens, having been born in Antwerp in 1599. His mother was noted for exquisite needle-work, disclosing in silk embroidery artistic skill and taste. Having herself taught Antony the rudiments, she placed him, at the early age of eleven, to study with Van Baelen, a former fellow-student of Rubens under Van Noort. At seventeen he entered the studio of the great Master.

Rubens, his day's work being done, had the custom in the afternoon to ride out on horseback for a couple of hours. One day, during his absence, the pupils, crowding round a freshly painted large picture, one of them was pushed against it, effacing the arm and chin of a Virgin. When their first consternation had subsided, Van Hoeck cried out : " Van Dyck is the handiest, he must repair the mischief." Van Dyck set to work so capably, that it is

said, Rubens, the next morning, did not at first
discover that there had been a strange hand
upon his canvas.

Van Dyck was precocious. Before he had
completed his twentieth year, he was admitted
to the Academy of Antwerp, the youngest
member ever entered on their rolls. While
still in the studio of Rubens he had already a
reputation. In the contract made with Rubens
by the Jesuits to paint thirty-nine pictures for
their church, it is agreed that the Master shall
do the sketches which are to be executed by
Van Dyck and his other scholars, the Master
to retouch and finish the whole. Of all the
scholars Van Dyck alone is mentioned by
name. An agent of the Earl of Arundel, writing to the Earl from Antwerp in 1620, when
the young painter was hardly twenty-one, says :
" Van Dyck lives with Rubens, and his works
begin to be almost as much esteemed as those
of his master."

Like Rubens, and at his recommendation,
Van Dyck went to Italy, and spent there five
years. He had less firmness of fibre, more
mobility and impressibility than Rubens, and
thence could not so staunchly assert and main-
tain his individuality. He adopted the man-

ner of those he admired. In Italy, and just
after his return, he painted pictures which, says
Michiels, one might take for Correggios, or
Titians or Paul Veroneses. Van Dyck has left
masterpieces in large pictures on sacred subjects, but it was in portraits that he excelled.
Many portraits he left in the palaces of Italy.
While preserving the likeness he had the gift
to impart to most heads a look of distinction,
—a rare facility, which came from the refinement of his genius, a native elegance of mind.
Happy are those of his contemporaries who
have the privilege of being handed down to
posterity by his pencil, and the list includes
warriors, nobles, cardinals, princes, citizens and
kings.

Van Dyck painted many more men than
women, and with more success. Frederick,
Prince of Orange, invited him to Holland to
take his likeness. While in Holland he called
to see a noted portrait painter, François Hals.
Hals being at a neighboring tavern, where he
spent much of every day in drinking and smok-
ing, the servant-maid ran to tell him that a
handsome young stranger was waiting for him.
When Hals arrived, Van Dyck told him that
he had come expressly to have his portrait

11

painted by so celebrated an artist, but that he had only two hours to spare. Hals snatched up his brush and set vigorously to work. Before the two hours were out he paused and asked the sitter how he liked his portrait? Van Dyck was warm in praise of it, but added, that he was an amateur, and it did not seem to him difficult to take a likeness : " let us change places and see what I can make of you." Hals gave him a fresh canvas, and Van Dyck handled the brush so rapidly and deftly, that Hals wondered at the readiness of a mere amateur. When at last he was asked to get up and look at his likeness, the moment his eyes rested on it, he exclaimed : " You are Van Dyck : no other painter in the world can paint such a portrait as that ; " and embraced him with enthusiasm.

In 1632 Van Dyck was invited to England by King Charles I. who received him with cordiality, gave him free lodgings both in town and country, a pension of £200, and for two years employed him continuously, as the disbursements on the treasury-registers prove. Michiels thinks that Van Dyck's liveliest admirations were for tyrants, heroes, and women. Four times he painted the beautiful Venetia

Stanley, the wife of his friend, Sir Kenelm
Digby. Drawn by the example of the King,
the nobility crowded his easel with portraits.
To-day, Windsor Castle and the seats of many
peers and gentlemen enjoy the luxurious fruit
of the admiration which Van Dyck's contemporaries had for him and his aristocratic bearing,
and manners. It was deemed a privilege to be
painted by him and to be his friend and patron.
The wealth that thence flowed in led Van
Dyck into luxurious habits. The asthetic nature, with its sensuousness and susceptibility,
tends towards sensual indulgence. The poetic
temperament of the artist, his mobility and his
very delicacy of perception, expose him to more
seductive temptations than men of less finely
tempered clay. Any excess is demoralizing, —
especially to these sensitive organizations, —
and when habitual, deteriorates by durably
relaxing all the fibres, the spiritual, the intellectual, the sensuous.

To replenish a purse drained by lavish house-
keeping and more lavish mistresses, Van Dyck
took advantage of his vogue and painted very
fast, having clever assistants to further him ;
and as if he were not going down hill rapidly
enough, he gave himself a kick, still to hasten

his speed, by partnership with alchemists and searchers for the philosopher's stone ; as wise therein as a modern spendthrift who tries to redeem himself by lottery-tickets.

The King, in the midst of his own trials, was a good friend throughout to Van Dyck, and gave proof that he was by bringing about a marriage between him and Mary Ruthven, the penniless beautiful daughter of an ancient house. This seems to have saved Van Dyck from ruin. He went back to Antwerp, but soon returned to England, to die there at the early age of forty-two.

Jacques Jordaens was, after Van Dyck, the most conspicuous among the pupils of Rubens. Pictures of his are still admired in the Louvre, at Antwerp, and elsewhere. He was a brilliant colorist and a painter of boldness and vigor, but he did not attain to the control of his powers and the harmony in execution, which in his master were the fruit of finer poetic sensibility. Jordaens was first a pupil of Van Noort, one of the teachers of Rubens, and, when very young, he fell in love with Van Noort's daughter, who consoled him for the rough treatment of the crabbed father. His marriage with her in 1616, when he was twenty-three, prevented him from going to Italy. He became a Protestant, which does not seem to have hurt his professional prosperity. He was prudent and diligent, accumulated property, and died at the age of eighty-five.

François Snyders, the famous painter of animals, was not a pupil of Rubens, but a personal friend and frequent partner. Born in 1579, he was two years younger than his friend. They worked harmoniously together, having much artistic as well as personal sympathy. Snyders did the animals and flowers in some of the pieces of Rubens; Rubens put in human figures into the hunts of Snyders. Snyders lived to be seventy-eight.

There were three Teniers, the father and two sons. We have here only to do with one, the most famous, David junior, a pupil, as his father had been, of Rubens, by whose genius he was warmed and advanced. At first he endeavored to follow Rubens into the higher regions of Art, but for this he had not the pinion. The *Kermess*, the landscapes and sketches of his great master were more profitable models for him. Here, says Michiels, " are the same tones, the same dexterity of the brush, the same lightness of touch. To Rubens he particularly owes his effects of color." Besides Rubens, another eminent artist had a profitable influence on Teniers : this was Adrian Brawer. Here is a fit place to relate how Brawer and Rubens first met.

To get rid of clamorous creditors Brawer left Amsterdam so suddenly, that he had no passport, and, war having just been renewed between Holland and Belgium, about the year 1634, when he presented himself at the gates of Antwerp, he was arrested and thrown into the citadel. It happened that, on account of a suspected conspiracy of the nobles in Belgium against Isabella, one of their chiefs, the Duke of Aremberg, was temporarily confined in the citadel. Having the freedom of the inclosure, the Duke, walking near the window of Brawer's cell, was accosted by Brawer, who, taking him for the Governor of the fortress, begged to be liberated, protesting he was not a spy but a painter, as he could prove if they would furnish him a canvas, colors and brushes. The Duke sent to Rubens for these articles. The joy of Brawer at getting hold of his familiar beloved tools was redoubled when a favorite subject presented itself in the shape of Spanish soldiers who, with their broad-brimmed hats and pict-

uresque costumes, planted themselves before
his window to play at cards and dice, their companions looking on. Brawer did his best, and
the sketch so pleased the Duke, that he sent
for Rubens, who, on seeing it, exclaimed ;
" That is the work of Brawer." Rubens obtained his release, gave him a fresh wardrobe,
and made him an inmate of his house. But to
a man of Brawer's temperament and habits, the
refinements and order of such a household are
an impertinence instead of a charm. He soon
took to the tavern again, wandered into France,
sank lower and lower, and returned to Antwerp to die in an obscure inn at the early age
of thirty-two.

Teniers was a realist, an admirable colorist,
and had, says one of his commentators, the
greatest among a painter's gifts, a mastery of
perspective. Productiveness is inherent in the
æsthetic realist ; witness Rubens and Goethe.
Nature, fact, palpable truth are enough for
them. To whatever they touch they impart
more or less poetic freedom ; but they are not
fastidious ; through delight in nature and movement, they are readily pleased with healthy
specimens, are not tormented with too exacting
ideals, as Leonardo da Vinci was, and Alston,

and Shelley. Teniers left a vast pictorial pro-
geny, so numerous, it is thought that picture-
dealers have given his name to hundreds of
pictures that were done by his father and
brother and by his scholars and imitators. He
lived to be eighty-four.

Rubens kept open house for scholars as well
as Artists. For science and literature he had
ever a learner's eye and ear. His correspondence with the celebrated Peiresc, the Mecænas
of his day, and with others, shows how real and
lively was his interest in learning and culture. Among the frequenters of his hospitable
home, in later years, was a handsome, graceful,
sprightly young man, a student of science and
philosophy. This was Erasmus Quellyn, who,
under influence of the personal attractiveness,
and professional prestige of Rubens, gave up
Philosophy for Art, and, through the instruction of his renowned friend, became one of his
most capable followers, resembling Van Dyck
in the poetic quality of his mind. Like him,
too, he became distinguished for portraits, in
which he approached so near to the excellence
of Van Dyck, that Michiels, — who seems to
have looked keenly into the matter, — believes
that to this day picture-dealers give Van Dyck's

name to many portraits done by the hand of
Quellyn. It **should be** stated that Michiels
thinks so highly of Quellyn, he lifts him into
the first rank of Artists. He was a man of
strong religious feelings, and put a more exalted
expression than his **great. master** into pious subjects. On public **occasions,** when triumphal
arches and painted decorations were wanted **in**
Antwerp, Quellyn was employed **to execute**
them, assisted by the learned, accomplished
Gaspard Gevaerts, the nephew and friend of
Rubens, who much valued him. Having lost
his wife in his latter years, Quellyn retired to
the **convent** of Tougaloo, where he died in 1678,
aged seventy-one.

Michiels calls Jean Van Hoeck one of the
best **pupils of** Rubens, and opens a notice of
him as follows : " Like Erasmus Quellyn, J.
Van Hoeck **seems** to me a superior painter, who
has been unjustly allowed to fall **into oblivion.**
Among a people without literature **and without**
critics, many a **man** may **thus die** a second
death." Besides **the** continuous inward fruition
which the gifted mind has from its gifts, the
career of Van Hoeck well illustrates what a
favor of fortune it was in those days to possess
artistic power. Born in **1598, in** Antwerp, of

well-to-do parents in good position, who gave him the best education then to be had, he cultivated his faculties by study of science and literature before he took up the pallet.   In due time he went to Rome, where at first he worked in seclusion.   But ere long his merit was discovered, and orders flowed in fast upon him, from cardinals and nobles.   They wished to keep him in Rome, but the Emperor Ferdinand II., invited him to Germany, where he passed the better part of his life, painting for churches and chateaus.   Having a strong desire to see his native land, he went back in 1647, and died, only three years later, in Brussels. "Odious death touched him with its lethargic wand, and put him to sleep the eternal sleep." Sentences like this, — not unfrequent in the pages of Michiels, — dispose one to think at times that, in spite of his marked merits of industry and insight, he is too much addicted to rhetorical exaltation to be at all times perfectly trustworthy.

From Holland Rubens also drew pupils. Theodore van Thulden, Abraham van Diepenbeck, and Juste van Egmont were Hollanders. Switzerland furnished Samuel Hofman.   Towards the end of his life the impoverishment

of Belgium, from war, oppression, and **bad government**, increased. Artists got few orders,
except the Antwerp master : and most of his
came from abroad. Like Van Dyck and
Hoeck, other of his pupils resorted to foreign
lands for work. Among these a good landscape painter, François Wouters, went to
England. Juste van Egmont prospered in
France.

Besides pupils, Rubens had **a** crowd of rivals
and imitators. Of these, the reader curious to
know about them, will find details, often interesting, in the volume of Michiels, who has
been at great pains to disengage their lives
and work from **the** misstatements of careless
or ignorant biographers.

XI.

FELLOW-FEELING is a quickener of insight. Antipathy is blinding, sympathy enlightening. When we hate a man, we do not know him so well as when we love him. When we are partial *for* him, our partiality carries us up into light: partiality *against* him bears us down into the dark. In drawing from some of the commentators on Rubens, in order to help myself and my readers to a fuller view of him, I shall use those pages that are brightened by the glow of admiration, — brightened, because the admiration seems to be judicious.

The first citation is but a single line, but it is a weighty line, coming from a contemporary, and a great contemporary. The Marquis Spinola, commander of the Spanish forces in the Netherlands, the formidable military rival of Prince Maurice, was one of the chief promoters of the truce of 1609, and when, twelve years later, it expired, he agreed with Rubens in wishing to see the truce converted into a peace.

In the protracted negotiations of several years, Isabella, Spinola, and Rubens formed a harmonious humane trio for peace, against the senseless inhumanity and obstinacy of Spain. By the side of Isabella, and elsewhere, Spinola and Rubens met in frequent confidential intercourse; and Spinola, — one of the master-spirits of the age, then of wide public experience, qualified as few are to judge of high men, and especially of the qualities of his eminent colleague, — said of him : " Painting is the least of the merits of Rubens." In these memorable words are we not justified in seeing a tribute to the great heart of the man as well as to his great intellect ?

The next judgment we cite is likewise a short one and equally significant, uttered by another great man, and one whose opinion on Art and artists is as that of the chief of a Court of highest resort, his decision being next to irreversible. Goethe, in his essay, " Ancient and Modern," brings forward Rubens in support of the position, that Art, to achieve its best, requires favorable outward circumstances. " Let us consider," says Goethe, " the immense stride made by the highly gifted Rubens, into the world of Art! He too was no son of earth."

Rubens has been compared to Scott, to Dryden, to Shakespeare. Such comparisons are apt to be made superficially, as easy helps to analysis, and stand mostly on spindle legs with loose joints. If anything is to be gained from such juxtaposition of proficients in different fields of Art, a parallel might be run between Rubens and Goethe. In mental structure and in performance they were much alike. Both were realists, in the sense that both accepted and entirely enjoyed nature, and had quick loving eyes to perceive her meaning and her infinite diversity of forms ; nor did either of them seek to better her by transcendental subjective imaginings. In the organization of both there was fondness for individualities and details combined with generic breadth. Both were incessant workers, with an exuberance of vitality, that was ever urgent for discharge : and thus both threw off much that had not the closeness of thought or finish of execution that the best products of Art should have ; except that in execution Goethe was at all times well nigh faultless. Like Goethe, Rubens wisely admired the Ancients, and like him drew largely from their legends and mythologies. They readily lent their genius to the adorn-

ment of temporary festivals. On the entrance
of the Regent Ferdinand into Antwerp, in
1635, Rubens, growing old, furnished elaborate
designs for eleven triumphal arches, among
them one of his most spirited poetic conceptions, — War issuing out of the temple of
Janus, the door pulled open by the Furies.
Goethe did like service at Weimar for **royal**
visits and birthdays ; both doing this **subordi-**
nate duty well and willingly, from the combination in both of facility of work with respect **for**
Princes. Each of them became the esteemed
confidential adviser of his Sovereign ; both
giving proof of sound capacity for statesman-
ship. Neither seems to have been self-tor-
mented by envy and jealousy. Each the favor-
ite of Princes and Princesses, the handsome,
graceful courtier, the captivating talker, the
welcome guest in the best companies, each was
ever cool and clear-sighted in work-day **prac-**
tice, hard to circumvent in great things **or**
small. In a rare degree genius and **common**
sense were united in Rubens as in Goethe.
M. Eugene Fromentin says, "the rapture of
Rubens is an exalted common sense." In public, **brilliant,** showy men of the world, the cyn-
osure of all eyes, in private both were as hard,

methodical workers as the most industrious of
day-drudges. Each a man of many sides, each
was liable to be misjudged by the one-sided,
especially by the pharisees. And this is still a
trouble with both ; or rather, it is a trouble
with some of their commentators.

German criticism, so rich in all departments,
makes various mention of Rubens. Raumer's
" Historisches Tashenbuch" for 1856, has a
long, thorough paper on his diplomatic career,
among the notes to which the following judgment is quoted from Füssli's "Kritisches Ver-
zeichniss der besten Kupferstiche" : " Rubens
was one of those extraordinary men who appear
only in the course of centuries. The history of
modern Art can scarcely present a painter (Raphael excepted), whose genius was so comprehensive, whose imagination was so creatively
rich, whose understanding was so cultivated
and enlightened by knowledge and science, and
with whom eye and hand were so responsive
to knowledge and will as with Rubens."

Dr. Waagen, who is an authority in Art-criti-
cism, and from whose volume, " Peter Paul Rubens, his Life and Genius," we have been glad
to quote, furnishes to this chapter the following
valuable passage : " A most glowing and crea-

tive fancy, inexhaustible in the conception of new forms full of life and vigor, would naturally find even the easiest method of painting tedious, and thus feel the necessity of acquiring some method of transferring its creations to the canvas in the shortest time possible. His rare technical skill, and his extraordinary faculty of color, aided Rubens admirably in attaining this object. He obtained at once the art of placing with a master hand, the right tones in the right places, without trying all kinds of experiments with the colors on the pictures themselves ; and after he had with ease blended them together, he knew how to give to the whole picture the last finish by a few master touches in those parts which he had left unpainted for the purpose. This mode of treatment, so characteristic of the turn of Rubens's mind, is the reason why his pictures bear the stamp of an original lively burst of fancy more than those of any other painter. Hence Rubens, beyond any artist of modern times, may be styled a sketcher in the highest and best sense of the word. If the greater part of his pictures bear upon the whole the character of a cheerful jovial spirit, undisturbed by outward misfortunes, and a strong feeling of complacency,

still these qualities are more particularly expressed in the style of his coloring.   Rubens,
as a colorist, might be called the painter of
light, as Rembrandt is the painter of darkness.
With Rubens everything is imbued with the
pure element of broad light; the different
colors are brought close together in luxuriant
contrast; but in their harmonious relation to
each other they celebrate a common triumph.
Thus many of his large pictures, for instance,
the *Assumption of the Virgin*, in the Cathedral
of Antwerp, may be said to produce the same
effect as a symphony, in which the united
sounds of all the instruments blend together
joyously, divinely, mightily.   No other painter
has ever known how to produce such a full and
satisfactory tone of light, such a deep *chiaro
oscuro*, united with such general brilliancy.
Few can be compared to him in the admirable
gradations in the keeping of the whole, and in
the manner in which each variety of surface is
distinctly pronounced; the coloring of his flesh,
in particular, has such a vivid transparency of
tone, such a glow of life, that it is easy to understand how Guido Reni should have been
struck with wonder upon beholding a picture
of Rubens's for the first time."

So many works of Rubens's being in England, he is there well known, and has been often written about. Thackeray, himself a pictorial as well as verbal artist, is not an admirer of the renowned Fleming, and in hasty language utters, in his " Roadside Sketches," what may be called crude judgments upon him. But a portrait in the Brussels Gallery he makes the object of enthusiastic eulogy : " The picture to see here is a portrait, by the great Peter Paul, of one of the governesses of the Netherlands. It is just the finest portrait that ever was seen. Only a half-length, but such a majesty, such a force, such a splendor, such a simplicity about it ! The woman is in a stiff black dress, with a **ruff**, and **a** few pearls ; a yellow curtain is **behind her,** — the simplest arrangement that can **be** conceived. But this great man knew how **to** rise to his occasion ; and no better proof can be shown of what a **fine gentleman** he was than this his homage to **the** vice-queen. A common bungler would have painted her in her best clothes, with crown and sceptre, just **as our** queen has been painted by — but comparisons are odious. Here stands this majestic **woman in** her every-day working-dress of black satin, *looking your hat off*, as it were.

Another portrait of the same personage hangs elsewhere in the gallery, and it is curious to observe the difference between the two, and see how a man of genius paints a portrait, and how a common limner executes it."

A good critic writes, in the " Edinburgh Review" for January, 1863, an article on the volumes of Sainsbury and Gachet. I can only afford room for one extract : " In his pictures of women, Rubens was curiously unequal. Some of them inspire both aversion and regret, others again are exceedingly noble and stately, although the Flemish type be one which does not admit of the tenderest refinement. In the *Virgin taught to read by St. Anna,* which hangs in the Antwerp Museum, the girl in her white lustrous robe, is both delicately imagined and beautifully painted, and the remembrance of those shy maiden glances is not easily effaced. Beautiful, too, is the Magdalen, among *The Four Penitents,* at Munich ; and still more is the *St. Theresa,* pleading with eloquent hands and eyes for the souls in Purgatory ; while, in quite another style, nothing surpasses the *Chapeau de Paille,* and the lady (said to be Isabella Brandt), in the great *Wolf Hunt* of Lord Ashburton's collection. How well she

sits her horse at her husband's side, and they
seem, as they ride together out over the breezy
downs, with the great white clouds rolling over-
head, and the hunted creatures at their feet, to
have been truly some Lord and Lady of La
Garaye of Flemish Life! The horse in this
hunt is magnificent; and Rubens was never
more happy than in painting the animal he
loved; unless, indeed, when he gives us a group
of joyous children, dragging after them some
great garland of fruit and flowers; a branch of
his art which one must see *The Seven Boys* at
Munich, in order to appreciate and admire."

From Mr. Ruskin, — whose copious writings,
begun thirty years since, have done much in
England and America to raise the tone of Art-
criticism and to enlighten its judgments, — I
take a short passage on the landscape of Rubens: "Not so Rubens, who perhaps furnishes
us with the first instances of complete uncon-
ventional unaffected landscape. His treatment
is healthy, manly, and rational, not very affectionate, yet often condescending to minute and
multitudinous detail; always, so far as it goes,
pure, forcible and refreshing, consummate in
composition and marvellous in color."

Coleridge says of the power of thought and

color in Rubens, that a large masterpiece of
his is " one vast and magnificent whole, con-
sisting of heaven and earth and all things
therein."

Mrs. Jameson, by long study and love of Art,
a poetic temperament, clear intellect and rich
sensibility, has earned, through her several
superior books, a high place as expounder of
Art. From her preface to the English translation of Waagen's Life of Rubens is taken
the following instructive passage : " To venture
to judge Rubens, we ought to have seen many
of his **pictures.** His defects may be acknowledged once for **all** ; **they** are, in all senses gross,
open, palpable, — his florid color, dazzling and
garish in its indiscriminate excess ; his exaggerated redundant forms ; his coarse allegories ;
his historical improprieties ; his vulgar and
prosaic versions of the loftiest and most delicate creations of poetry, — let all these be
granted ; but this man painted that sublime
History [a series of six pictures], almost faultless
in conception and in costume, **the** *Decius* in the
Lichtenstein Gallery. This man — who has
been called **unpoetical, and** who was a born
poet, if **ever** there was one — conceived that
magnificent epic, the *Battle of the Amazons ;*

that divine lyric, the *Virgin Mary*, trampling
Sin and the Dragon, in the Munich Gallery —
which might be styled a Pindaric Ode in honor
of the Virgin, only painted instead of sung ;
and those tenderest moral poems, the *St.
Theresa* pleading for the Souls in Purgatory,
and the little sketch of *War*, where a woman
sits desolate on the black wide heath, with dead
bodies and implements of war heaped in
shadowy masses around her, while, just seen
against the lurid streak of light left by the setting sun, the battle rages in the far distance.
In both these pictures, the moral and the sentiment are so exquisitely pure and true, and con-
veyed to the mind and to the heart with such
comprehensive and immediate effect, that they
might be compared to some of the sonnets of
Filicaja. Look at the thirteen hundred pictures
of his vehement and abounding fancy ; in great
part the work of his own right hand. In these
multifarious creations, embracing almost every
aspect of life and nature, what amazing versatility of power as displayed in the conception
of his subjects, — what fertility of invention in
their various treatment ! What ardent, breathing, blooming life, — what pomp and potency
of color and light, have been poured forth on

his canvas! If he painted heavy forms, has
he not given them souls, and animated them
with all his own exuberance of vitality and
volition? Whatever his personages enact, they
do with all the earnestness of the soul which
conceived, and all the energy of the hand which
formed them. Dr. Waagen dwells on the
dramatic power of Rubens as the first and
grand characteristic of his genius; and who
ever excelled him in telling a story? in con-
necting, by sympathetic action or passion, his
most complicate groups, and with them, in
spirit, the fascinated spectator? And though
thus dramatic in the strongest sense, yet he is
so without approaching the verge of what we
call theatrical. With all his flaunting luxuri-
ance of color, and occasional exaggeration in
form, we cannot apply that word to him. Le
Brun is theatrical: Rubens never. His sins
are those of excess of daring and power; but
he is ever the reverse of the flimsy, the artifi-
cial or the superficial. His gay magnificence
and sumptuous fancy are always accompanied
by a certain impress and assurance of power
and grandeur, which often reaches the sublime,
even when it stops short of the ideal."

Since, what may be called the revival of

French Art, — begun about fifty years since by
a return to Nature, — the French school of
painting has taken a foremost place in Europe ;
and criticism has kept abreast of this practical
excellence. We begin with passages from M.
Taine, marked by his characteristic dash and
culture, audacity and insight, by his material-
istic tendency, and his guiding critical dogma
of the predominating importance of the *milieu ;*
" Among these painters, there is one who
seems to efface the rest ; indeed, no name in
the history of Art is greater, and there are only
three or four as great. But Rubens is not an
isolated genius, the number, as well as the resemblance of surrounding talents showing that
the efflorescence of which he is the most beautiful emanation, is the product of his time and
people. . . . Rubens goes to mass every morning, and presents a picture in order to obtain
indulgences ; after which he falls back on his
own poetic feeling for natural life, and, in the
same style, paints a lusty Magdalen and a
plump siren ; under the Catholic varnish the
heart and the intellect, all social ways and ob-
servances, are pagan."

Gustave Planche — one of the best of a good
class of recent French critics on Literature and

Art — has a breadth and liberality, together
with a fine natural cultivated perception, which
make his discussions and opinions attractive
and impressive. From the paper on Rubens,
in the volume, " Études sur les Arts," I extract two passages. After setting forth the rare
merits of the *Crucifixion of St. Peter*, the purity
of the drawing as well as its vigor, the delicacy
of modelling combined with Rubens's habitual
splendor, he continues : " That the **forms**
chosen **by** Rubens do not please all eyes, I
readily conceive ; that in his compositions
strength shows itself oftener than grace, is a
truth long recognized ; that more than once he
has sacrificed contour to color, cannot **be**
denied ; but he did not do this through ignorance. If he preferred splendor to precision,
he by no means had for purity of lines the
contempt which has been too often attributed
to him. He fully knew the importance of
drawing and had studied it zealously ; only he
had a way of seeing and rendering **nature**
which belonged to him, **and** which **gave to all**
his personages **a special character.** Among
his numerous detractors many a one takes his
originality for a proof of ignorance. He has
proved over and over again that he knew all

the secrets of the human form, but never has
he proved it so clearly as in the *Crucifixion of
St. Peter.* The elegance of St. John and of
Salomé, the whole trunk of the Christ in the
Descent from the Cross, may be cited as brilliant
evidences of knowledge. In this immortal
work there is a purity of lines which could not
but satisfy the severest taste ; even the legs of
the Christ, the movement of which has caused
so much anger among those who think themselves the only ones who possess the secret of
linear harmony, do not seem to me to deserve
the censure with which they have been visited ;
for they are true in the dramatic sense and in
the anatomical sense. At the same time, the
Crucifixion of St. Peter proves still better the
injustice of the accusation to which I have referred."

Towards the end of the essay, M. Planche
thus speaks of the influence of Rubens and of
his leading traits: "The influence of Rubens
on the development of painting is not difficult
to determine. On all representations of human
nature he has impressed a character of life and
reality which before him painting did not know.
Looked at from this exclusive point of view,
his works present to us an entirely novel char-

acter. In the whole history of Art before the
seventeenth century, there is not a single picture that can be compared to his for truth
taken in the prosaic sense of the word. Rubens, profiting by the lessons of his predecessors, endeavored to show us flesh such as he
saw it, and, whatever be the doctrine to be de-
fended, it must be admitted that he attained his
aim. To mark his rank in history, to show
the new elements he has introduced into painting, it is thus that he must be looked at. As
painter of flesh, as interpreter of life, he has
no rival. Whatever may be thought of the
forms he has chosen and reproduced, the evidence obliges us to acknowledge, that before
him no one had expressed life with so much
energy."

The latest, but by no means the least, of
French critics on Rubens is M. Eugéne Fromentin, in the "Revue des Deux Mondes" for
January first and fifteenth, 1876. M. Fromentin is himself a painter, and, if he paints as
well as he writes, a distinguished painter. His
descriptions of some of the principal works of
Rubens are as rich in color, as bold, and as
facile in execution as the pictures they describe.
As, like them, they cover a large space, I se-
lect two or three passages for translation.

" Scarcely have we set foot in the first hall of the Museum of Antwerp than **Rubens** welcomes us : to the right, an *Adoration of the Magi*, an immense picture in his rapid and **learned** manner, painted, it is said, in thirteen days, about 1624, that is, in the best years of his maturity ; to the left, a very large picture, also celebrated, a crucifixion called *The thrust of the lance*. We cast a look into **the gallery** which faces us, and on the right, on **the left**, we perceive afar this unique handiwork, strong and sweet, unctious and warm, — Rubenses, and after them still Rubenses. We begin with catalogue in hand. **Do** we always admire ? Not always. Do we remain cold ? Hardly ever.

" I write out my notes : the *Magi*, fourth version beginning with Paris, this time with notable alterations. This picture is less scrupulously studied than that of Brussels, less perfect as a whole than that of Malines, **but of** a greater boldness, of a breadth, of a fullness, of a confidence and self-possession which the painter has rarely surpassed in his calm productions. It is truly a *tour de force*, especially **if one recalls the** rapidity of this work of improvisation. **Not a gap, not a strain ; a vast**

clear half-tint and lights without excess envel-
op all the figures, supporting one the other;
all the colors are visible and multiply values
the most rare, the least sought and yet the most
fit, the most subtle and yet the most distinct.
By the side of types that are very ugly swarm
superior types. With his square face, his thick
lips, his reddish skin, big eyes strangely lighted
up, and his stout body girt in green pelisse with
sleeves of peacock blue, this African among
the Magi is a figure entirely new, before which
assuredly Tintoret, Titian, Veronese would
have clapped their hands. On the left stand
in dignified solemnity two colossal cavaliers,
of a singular Anglo-Flemish style, the most extraordinary piece of color in the picture, with
its dull harmony of black, greenish blue, of
brown and white. Add the profile of the
Nubian camel-drivers, the supernumeraries, men
in helmets, negroes, the whole in the most
ample, the most transparent, the most natural
of atmospheres. Spider-webs float in the
frame-work, and quite low down the head of
the ox, — a sketch achieved by a few strokes
of the brush in bitumen, — without more
importance and not otherwise executed than
would be a hasty signature. The child is de-

licious, to be cited as one of the most beautiful
among the purely picturesque compositions of
Rubens, the last word of his knowledge as
color, of his skill as technic, when his sight
was clear and instantaneous, his hand rapid
and careful, and when he was not too exacting,
the triumph of rapture and science — in a word,
of self-confidence."

From a page on Rubens as portrait-painter
is translated the following passage : —

" If to all the portraits he has painted sepa-
rately to satisfy the desire of his contemporaries,
— kings, princes, lords, doctors, abbes, priors, —
be · added the countless number of living personages whose features he has reproduced in
his pictures, it might be said that Rubens
spent his life in making portraits. His best
works undoubtedly are those in which the
greatest part is given to real life : witness his
admirable picture of *Saint George*, in the
church of St. James at Antwerp, which is nothing other than a votive family offering, that is
to say, the most magnificent and the most
curious document that ever painter left on his
domestic affections. I don't speak of his portrait of himself, of which he was so profuse,
nor of that of his two wives, of which he made,

as is known, so continual and so indiscreet a
use.

" To make use of nature on all occasions, to
take individuals in real life and introduce them
into his fictions, was with Rubens a habit because it was one of his needs, a weakness as
well as a strength of his mind. Nature was
his large and inexhaustible repertory. What
did he truly seek in nature? Subjects? No ;
his subjects he borrowed from history, from
legends, from Scripture, from fable, and always
more or less from his imagination. Attitudes,
movements, expressions of countenance ? No ;
these came naturally out of himself, and sprang,
by the logic of a well-conceived subject, out of
the necessities of the almost always dramatic
action which he had to produce. What 'he
asked of nature was what his imagination furnished him but imperfectly when there had to
be presented a person living from head to feet,
living in so far as he required it — I mean traits
more personal, characteristic qualities more
definite, individuals and types. These types,
he accepted them more than he selected them.
He took them such as they existed around
him, in the society of his time with all its ranks,
in all classes, if need be, in all races, — princes,

men of the sword, men of the church, monks, professional people, blacksmiths, boatmen, above all men of hard labor. There was in his own city, on the quays of the Schelde, enough to supply all the wants of his large scriptural pictures. He had a lively feeling of the relation these people, fresh from life, bore to the proprieties of his subject. When the fitness was not very exact, — what happened often, — and that good sense protested faintly, and even good taste, the love of details carried it against the proprieties, taste, and good sense."

From these eloquent pages of M. Fromentin, the noble tribute of genius to genius, I make one more extract : —

"About fifteen hundred works were painted by Rubens : this is the most immense production that ever issued from one brain. To approach this figure, we should have to add one to the other the life of several men among the most prolific producers. If, independently of the number, one considers the importance, the dimension, the complication of his works, we have a spectacle which confounds us, and which gives us the most elevated, let us say, the most religious idea of human faculties. Such at least seems to me to be the lesson which results from the amplitude and the power of a soul. In this respect he is unique ; and in every way he is one of the grandest specimens of humanity. In our Art we have to go up to Raphael, to Leonardo, to Michelangelo, up to the demi-gods, to find his equals, and, on certain sides, even his superiors. Nothing was wanting to him, it has been said, but the very pure instincts and the very noble. One could find indeed in the world of the beautiful two or three spirits who went further, who took a higher flight, who consequently got a nearer view of the divine lights, and the eternal truths. And in the moral world, in that of sentiments, of visions, of dreams, there are depths into which only Rembrandt has descended, into which Rubens has not penetrated and which he has not even perceived. On the other hand, he took possession of the earth as no other has. Sights are of his domain. His eye is the most wonderful of the prisms which have ever given us the light and the color of things, of ideas magnificent and true. The dramas, the passions, the attitudes of bodies, the expressions of countenances, that is to say, the whole man in the manifold incidents of human life, all this passes through his brain, puts on there

stronger features, **more** robust **forms, enlarges**
itself a little, does **not** refine itself **there but**
transfigures **itself into I** know not what **heroic**
appearance. He impresses upon everything
the distinctness of his character, the warmth
of his blood, the solidity of his stature, the admirable equilibrium of his nerves, and the
grandeur of his ordinary visions. He is unequal and exceeds measure ; he wants taste
sometimes when he draws, never when **he**
colors. He forgets himself, is careless, but
he always makes up for an error by a masterpiece ; he redeems a want of care, of seriousness,
of taste, by the instantaneous evidence of
respect for himself, of an almost touching ap-
plication, and a supreme judgment.

" The grace of Rubens is that of a man who
sees largely and strongly, and the smile of such
a man is delicious. When he puts his hand **on**
a subject which is **not** common, when **he**
handles a feeling that is profound and clear,
when his heart beats with a high and sincere
emotion, he executes the *Communion of St.
Francis of Assise*, and then in the class of conceptions purely moral, he attains to what is
most beautiful in the true, and he is thereby as
great as any **one in the world."**

XII.

FROM the foregoing pages the reader will, I trust, have been enabled to see Rubens as he was in his living aims and daily doings. To complete the attempted representation, it will be well to review some of his prominent traits, and present in a final judgment his intellectual and moral characteristics.

Rubens was a great artist. To be a great artist, a man must have great qualities in his mind. The gifted painter re-creates the best of humanity. The heroic, the pathetic, the most expressive conjunctions of life and history, all these he reproduces through the language of passionate color and life-like bodily movement ; and this he does so vividly, with such an art, as to impress the beholder with an exalted notion of the reality, thus animating, enlarging, refining our perceptions and sensibilities. The artist's function — what a high one ! — is to give us the best, and the best expression, of what is true and beautiful. His

business is, to put before us captivating significant pictures of the actualities and possibilities
of life.

To be able to project your conceptions into
definite buoyant corporeality is a high and rare
gift. Try to draw and color a single head,
and see how near you will come to it; then
add the limbs and trunk to the head; **then**
set your head and body in motion; then com-
bine their motion with that of others, of many,
so as to express clearly and attractively a sentiment, an act, an event. This is a grand exhibition of human powers, and when exerted
to express **noble** touching deeds and feelings,
is the achievement of a man admirable and
superior through his faculties of perception,
judgment and sensibility, and who, through his
faculty of representing and interpreting, in
shining colored surfaces and shapes, what is
most true in human life, what is at once speci-
fic and generic, is a great painter.

How fond all people are of pictorial illustrations: to all they appeal with such sensuous
liveliness. Let them show, not imagination
merely, — for the baldest most prosaic of them
necessarily **do that,** — but *poetic* imagination,
that is, some **feeling for** the beautiful in form

and sentiment, and you have Art. I have an edition of Tristram Shandy of 1780, with six illustrations. Four of them give you no help ; they are not *illustrations*, for they throw no fresh lustre on the book, are almost as flat and unprofitable as would be the *Allegro* translated into prose. Two are by Hogarth, and these two add life to the text. Seizing the subtler sense of his author, by grouping and expression he reanimates the page. He cheers us with a pleasant and profitable mental stimulus ; we thank him for a favor done us. A copy of the " Divina Commedia," with a running commentary of sketches by Michelangelo, is said to have been lost at sea : there was an illuminated manuscript! In most illustrations there is a deep defect : they do not illustrate ; the figures have shapely bodies, but no souls. Would that we had some pictorial comments by Rubens on his contemporary, Shakespeare.

Could it have happened that he had seen Macbeth, or King John or Lear, his devouring eye would have feasted on scenic groups that would have given the substance of pictures for his canvas. The majestic countenance of Shakespeare, (what an invitation to a great painter !) that he had not the privilege of beholding, for

Rubens arrived first in England in 1629, and a dozen years before this date, his mighty compeer, having finished the work allotted to him on earth, had ascended to higher spheres. What a picture Rubens would have made of Lear on the heath, encompassed by flashes of lightning, with the faithful fool crouching near him ; or of Macbeth, when Banquo " with his throat cut," is so unmannerly as to appear at the banquet. But it is idle to multiply subjects for Rubens : he could himself multiply them fast enough. Aye, and too fast, say some.

The fertility and rapidity of Rubens, — distinctions which he shares with Raphael, with Albert Durer, with Velasquez, besides Shakespeare and Goethe, — are at times made a reproach to him. Some reproductive natures are so happy in a bursting fullness of material, that they must be incessantly bringing forth : with them, to live is to produce. None of their light can be hid under a bushel : mankind must have the benefit of the whole of it, though often they cannot take time to purge their flames of all grosser elements. As to Rubens, it seems to me that M. Gustave Planche says of him justly : " Fully to reveal himself, he needed to multiply his works, to express his power through forms unceasingly renewed. For **cer-tain** minds, even of the most elevated **order,** **slowness is a** necessity ; for other minds, of an **equal** rank, slowness would only be an unprofit-able suffering, and Rubens was one of these."

This fertility spread his handiwork wherever Art was valued. Now, suppose one thousand of his pictures rejected and destroyed, only the best being preserved ; there would still be left two or three hundred, which connoisseurs and ardent lovers of Art would congregate to con-tend **for the** possession of, whenever one of them **should** happen to emerge, and come within grasp, — two **or** three hundred master-pieces, more or less, ranging in subject over the whole domain of pictorial Art. This fourth part only of the treasures that were scattered over Europe from that inexhaustible mint, his studio, would be a bequest to the world as pre-cious as that of any of his superlative rivals, as rich in choice specimens, and richer than any in their profusion and variety, the greater part of them exemplifying the vigorous æsthetic prin-ciple, — as imperative in the best pictorial as **in the** best literary Art, — that not only should the conception of the whole have a rounded poetic life, but the limbs and parts should be moulded **so in** unison with the **demands of the** beautiful that there be nothing prosaic, **all** the lines true and pure, just as in an excellent poem there should be no prosaic line. What is a prosaic line? This is not an irrelevant question here ; the poetic requirements are similar in the two arts.

When Hamlet, on recognizing Marcellus, says :

"I am very glad to see you. **Good even, Sir** " ;

and a few lines further to Horatio, —

"I think it was to see my mother's wedding " :

these are not prosaic lines ; to ordinary unelevated feeling or thought they give the best form of words desirable or possible. Big words and the sweep of sounding rhythm would be out of place ; but there is a rhythm, as there is to every speech and passage of this vivid scene, as there is to every speech and passage written by Shakespeare. His music is **an inward part** of his poetry. However matter-of-fact **the** statement, or plain the words and form, these never fall below the demand of the moment. **A line is** prosaic when it does fall below this demand, when the utterance, the embodiment, **is not** so high **as the** thought **or** feeling and occasion admit of. **Let** Horatio open the account of the Ghost's appearance to Marcellus and Bernardo, thus:

> For two night's in succession had these two,

instead of as it stands,—

> "Two nights together had these gentlemen,"

and you substitute a prosaic line for one that is not prosaic. The line substituted falls below the capability of the occasion. In its spring and movement it is not in harmony with the other lines of the animated scene. Observe: we say, the line as it stands in Shakespeare, is not prosaic ; we do not say it is poetical. In a long poem you are lucky, as Lord Byron says, if now and then you get a poetic sparkle. Such we do get in the third line of Horatio's narration,—

> "In the dead vast and middle of the night."

It should be observed, too, that mere metre will not save a line from falling below the demands of the occasion. Metre is the necessary machinery to the body of a poem ; the soul is in the rhythm. Nor is metre, that is, regular cadence, necessary to either rhythm or poetry. Is there, even in Shakespeare, a deeper, more significant, a fuller, more poetical or grandly rhythmical passage than that in the second scene of the second Act of Hamlet, beginning:

"I have of late — **but** wherefore I know not — lost all my mirth"?

And yet it is prose in form. Genius makes its caprices seem the result of profound law.

Now, in painting, what is a prosaic line or color? Any one which falls below the demand of its place; any one which is not so pure as the occasion will admit of. Look at only an engraving of one of Rubens's capital pictures; there is rhythm in the lines, there is poetry in the grace and symmetrical diversity in the unconfused complexity of curves, in their wonderfully harmonious combination.

And those thousand that were supposed destroyed, the larger part of which happily still survive: is there not in them much of this magical play of curve and colors? Have they not upon them, to those who can read it, the superscription of a master-mind? Take them down from the walls of their homes in the Palaces, the Cathedrals, the Galleries, the mansions of Italy, Spain, France, England, Belgium, Holland, Germany, Russia, and a wide chasm would be made in the aureole that glorifies the head of European civilization; and there would be **grief as for** the loss of a valued friend of a **family, often as for that of a** cherished inmate.

The life of thought is in every one of them;
and in some form, either of invention, grouping,
color, individual excellence, there are beams
from the unfathomable soul of the beautiful.
To each has been imparted, by the hand of
genius, some of that glow which is only kindled
by that creative look which sees lights in nature
only seen by the gifted. The longer a poetic
mind gazes at a chosen subject, the more does
the subject sparkle with life, the more does its
inward spirit gleam out, to enlighten it, to beau-
tify it, as by the shining of the sun on the earth
the earth grows blooming and golden with the
buoyancy of foliage and the weight of ripeness.
The fructifying look of genius has not dwelt
long enough on them to draw out their sweetest juices, but there is on the least of them a
stamp from the seal which can only be heated
in celestial fire, in them some of the breath of
Art's life, which is the beautiful. Beauty is
the bride of life. Put life into a work of Art
and you will have more or less of beauty: the
two cannot be divorced. Wherever there is
life there is beauty; wherever there is beauty
there is life.

Much unconsidered talk has been and is in-
dulged in about the coarseness and glare and

haste of Rubens. Rubens had faults, for he was a **man, and** palpable faults ; but many beholders pass by a picture for its faults, which are obvious, and fail to discern its virtues, which are less obvious.

Let us attribute this vast, this unprecedented multiplication of pictures chiefly to the prolific activity of a large brain, to exuberance **of re**source, to rich spontaneousness. The renown and facility of Rubens tempted him, **with the** aid of apt pupils, to force at times his productive power for the gold which followed its exer**cise** ; but this, a partial, fractional motive, should not be set down as the foremost cause of the multiplication. Rubens valued gold, not like a miser, for itself, or like a speculator, for its controlling power " on 'change," but for the solid utilities, the intellectual and spiritual enjoyments, that are to be had for it. We **have** seen how he spent upon his Art-collection ; how from brother artists he purchased their works. Van Dyck, when he came **back** from Italy, found little sale for his pictures. Not being of so robust a moral nature as his master **and friend, he** was depressed. Rubens went to **his studio and** comforted him, and bought all **that were finished. The same** he did to one of

his contemporaries and **rivals, an artist** of
merit, but whose works accumulated upon his
hands, chiefly because of the overshadowing
reputation of Rubens. His pencil not serving
him in competition with his renowned neighbor,
he used his tongue malignantly against him.
Notwithstanding this, Rubens paid him a visit,
was courteous and kind, went through his
studio, and gave full prices for many of **his**
works. Rubens had many sides to him ; here
he showed his Franklin side. When Jean
Breughel, — with whom he formed a life-friend-
ship in Italy, — died in 1625, Rubens took
upon himself the guardianship and education of
his orphan daughters, and fulfilled the trust
with fidelity and tenderness.

There is a difference, — a difference as of
night and day, — between a self-seeker and a
man who seeks to unfold himself fully as man
and artist. Your self-seeker uses you to help
him up that ladder which he never lets go,
which he ever hugs, waking or sleeping, and of
which he never reaches the top, — worldly
ascent, a ladder which is the opposite of Jacob's,
for, while it seems to carry you finally up, it is
in fact carrying you down. To get tighter
hold on one of its rounds, the self-seeker will,

if need be, trample you in the mud, or empty
you of all you own. Whereas, the man who
seeks to cultivate, to unfold himself, takes no
more from you than one candle does from
another when lighting itself at a flame: he
seeks more light, and, while drawing from
yours, adds to it. He is mounting Jacob's ladder, and angels are helping him.

Here, again, the parallel holds between Rubens and Goethe. Neither was an ambitious
self-seeker, narrowly using his fellows for his
profit; but each broadly used them for his and
for theirs. With them, ambition, worldly elevation were secondary; self-improvement, intellectual and moral culture, primary. Being
persistent and practical, as well as of rare
ableness and activity, their self-improvement
brought honors, gold, reputation, position, full-
est worldly success. This they accepted as
their due; but they did not primarily seek it,
or go aside out of the straight upward path to
compass it. In this both were exemplars of an
upright healthy manhood.

When Marie dei Medici postponed payment
for the long series he had painted for her,
Rubens grew impatient, and wrote to one of
his learned French correspondents, " I am sick

of this **Court.**" Rubens, **like** Goethe, was a thorough man **of** business, methodical, regular, punctual. This side of his nature was not a mere ballast to steady his genius ; it was the muscle and bone, the sustaining mates to the nerves : it gave his upper powers hinges for their full swing. Meeting Rubens in a company of men of the world, he would have been taken for one of the shrewdest of them, — **an** impression **such** as Wordsworth made on **Jeff-**rey when they first met **at a** London dinner-party. Rubens was **a** hard worker who did not brook being put off for his well-earned pay, **especially** not, we venture to affirm, by idle **people who** do not **know** what hard work is. Had Rubens, instead of being many-sided, been one-sided, a man of narrow range, his love of accumulation might have turned into a vice, and made him lop-sided ; but this love was in him one of many loves that worked together and gave strength to one another, and helped to harmonize his many-sidedness. It did its part in moving him **to get** full service out of **his** fine powers.

Rubens **had in** him not only the rare gifts for genial achievement, but the still rarer faculty of wise self-guidance. It has been shown

how in boyish days **he** withstood the **fascina-**
tions of courtly luxurious life, and gave up being
page to a noble lady to become a drudge in the
studio. Could we surely follow his early steps,
it would probably be discovered, that chiefly
by personal self-direction **he** passed from one
teacher to another, until he reached the sympathetic Venius. From the first he had a distinct
perception of the best means to the **end** pro-
posed ; and his chief ends were high. He
went to Spain for his liberal patron Gonzaga,
because the mission suited his personal aims
and furthered him on his chosen pathway ; but
he declined to return through France, because
that journey would not minister to his own
plans. In the account of this mission to Spain,
M. Villaamil, commenting on one of the first
letters that Rubens wrote back to Mantua,
says : "How this letter reveals Rubens, although **so young.** His pride, which is not ar-
rogant assumption, the profound sentiment **of**
his own worth, — which only the ignorant are
in the habit of condemning ; his determination
not to employ his talents except in the high re-
gion of Art and thought."

As important is it for a **man** to see and judge
himself aright, as to judge aright any other man

or thing or event about him ; nay, more important, inasmuch as by beholding himself as he
is, he becomes capable of more true and solid
adjustment to his place in the world, gets into
his proper place and holds it more firmly.
Under-estimation of himself is as fatal to a man
as over-estimation. To us it seems that Rubens's vision of himself was no way clouded by
the fumes of self-flattery. He knew himself,
and of course, therefore, he knew his superiority to those about him, not only as artist, but
as every-day man, who had a clearer, deeper
perception of the prosaic relations that make
up the body of public and private life. But
this knowledge was not shadowed by vanity or
arrogance. There was not in Rubens, any
more than in Goethe, that absorbing self-love
which leaves no room for love of others, and
stains the clean objective vision of men and
things.

In the mind, and thence in the doings, of
Rubens reigned the law of order, the most rad-
ical, and the most conservative of laws, that
which gives to all other laws and regulations
their efficiency, their very life, the law which
must lie active and immovable at the basis of
all prosperous being. Never was any man's

day more governed by that method which reaps from the hour its best harvest. Rubens was one of those happy men who love to work. Men are most of them born to love work, could they but work according to the deeper laws of order. For its own full play and easy function, the large, active, cultivated, various mind of Rubens required and made order for itself. The rule of his household (and every inmate was the happier for it) was as precise and imperative as that of a man of war.

He began his day by attending mass. Rubens was by nature conservative, in practice a conformist, and he was a dutiful son. His mother, whom he loved while she lived, and whose memory he cherished and venerated, had brought him up in strict observance of the rites of her church. All the forenoon he worked in the studio, resting a while before dinner, which was then a midday meal. After dinner, probably not hurried, he went to work again. This he could do by virtue of a robust highly-nerved organism, maintained in vigor by temperance. In his latter years he suffered from gout. As he stood while painting, he had the best kind of bodily exercise, that which is taken unconsciously, and simultaneously with

intellectual movement. In the afternoon, before sundown, he mounted a horse (he had superb horses, partly a present from the King of
Spain) for a gallop outside the walls, along the
Schelde or into the interior. The evening he
gave to his family, to reading, to correspondents, to conversation with friends and visitors.

   With Philip Rubens, the nephew who wrote
a biography of his uncle, we are disposed to
quarrel when he says, that Rubens, while painting, had a reader sitting near who read to him
from Plutarch or Seneca. The saying that you
cannot do two things at once, may not be
strictly true; but one of the things done must
be mechanical. A lady can talk and knit at
the same time, but if she dives below the surface of talk, the knitting will stop ; or she may
read a book and rock her infant's cradle, —
if there be left in the world anything so per-
versely against nature as a rocking cradle, —
but the book must not draw deeply upon the
reason or the feelings. As to moulding, through
the eye, the forms and colors of the *Elevation
of the Cross*, or of a Silenus, or of a lion, while,
through the ear, the thoughts of Seneca are
claiming the attention — that is a psycholog-
ical impossibility. Think of Shakespeare being

read to while working **Othello up** to the madness of jealousy, or while Beatrice and Benedic are loosing their wit upon each other. True, pictorial poetry is more sensuous than written ; **but** its creative movement comes from as deep inward sources. A much less thing than a picture of Rubens, demands, in order that it be well done, undivided, unbroken attention. A painter, busied on a portrait, will sometimes invite a third person to talk to his sitter, in order to get the sitter's mind fully and unconsciously into his face ; but if he himself listens, with only half **an** ear, the portrait will lose somewhat. **Just** before setting to work, to **read** or have read to you a good thought-weighted book, is inspiring; still more so is music. A symphony of Beethoven, well executed, would exalt a poet or painter to his best. The statement must have originated in that way : Rubens was sometimes read to *before* he began work.

Rubens was an enjoyer : he joyed in old books, in a gallant horse, in good talk, in old friends, **in a classical** passage, in children, in seeing **new places, in** animals, in men and all their passions, in women without being betrayed into erotic immoralities, in accumulating money, in spending it wisely and kindly. In his brain there was more than usual variety of aptitude, as well as intensity of life; and being of a sunny temperament, he fronted the multitudinous life without him cheerfully, meeting light with light; and when there was darkness, casting upon it some of the day of his inward illumination.

He was a happy man and, as must be, his happiness flowed from within. Fortunate was he, too, through life; and Fortune is by no means so blind as she is reported: she soon deserts him who knows not how to make the best of her gifts. Most fortunate was Rubens in the lively start he got, in his very first beginnings, in his birth, in his father, and especially in his mother. It is evident, moreover, that this high mother did not spoil her beautiful sparkling boy. To him personal beauty was a good fortune, which it is not to all its possessors. The weak in character, of either sex, are liable to be spoiled by it. To him it was a good, because the inward was in accord with the outward. His conduct and intellect fulfilled the promise made by his countenance and figure. In him, beauty was the announcement of rare gifts. In this again Goethe and Rubens were alike.

Quickness **at** learning and **readiness to be** taught will draw and attach the teacher to **the** pupil. Rubens was thus a favorite with all his teachers. The last of his pictorial masters, Venius, took him to his bosom. The Duke of Mantua evidently did the same; and Albert and Isabella, when he returned from Italy, showered on him favors which ended in warmest esteem and lasting friendship. All this proves the intelligence and geniality there was in the man; and more than that, it proves that there was a sound heart in him. Rubens was not admired merely : he was beloved.

The union of warm poetic imagination **with** rare memory and substantial common sense,— the interior capital for the artist to draw upon, — stood him also in good stead in intercourse with his fellows. The strong men he came in contact with, all soon learnt to value and admire him; those who were at all given to affection loved him. His active genial life was a daily light to many men. The path of his pupils was the clearer for it, of his friends, of neighbors, of his townsmen, of his countrymen, of his sovereigns, of the master minds among his contemporaries. His worldly success enabled him to live "like a Prince," as the phrase

is. Of the grandeur and refinement of his
abode, one may judge from his Gallery, which
contained, at his death, over three hundred
pictures, many by Titian, Paul Veronese, Tintoret, Van Dyck, and others, of course nothing
weak in it, and ninety by his own hand. In
his roomy, tasteful, superb mansion in Antwerp, or at his *chateau* of Steen near Malines,
where in his latter years he spent part of the
summer, the instructive, captivating, humane
man shone ever to give life and significance to
his surroundings. Those sixty orphan children,
appointed to bear torches at his crowded, gorgeous public funeral, are expressive of much.

> One day in the month of May, 1640, there
was unwonted gloom in Antwerp, a strange
palor in the air, as of a solar eclipse. A pall
of sadness lay on the quiet town : men gathered
in groups and spoke low : Rubens is dead !
The solemn words passed from street to street :
Rubens is dead ! The town seemed suddenly
emptied : there was stillness as of a corpse
when the soul has just fled. Rubens is dead !
The words passed to Malines, to Brussels, to
Ghent, to Bruges, into Holland, into France,
into Germany. Europe had lost one of its
lights. Men felt awed. When a great man

dies, death is magnified : his ever impending stroke falls with a might that brings him home to the soul with an emphasis which seems to threaten all humanity. When the news reached Spain, the grave Spaniards grew graver ; and then quickly looked up at his pictures, as if to hold them fast, thankful that they had so much of Rubens. And when the tidings came to Italy, from Genoa, through Mantua, and Milan, and Venice, and Bologna, and Florence to Rome went the wail, from all the beautiful land he loved ; and Italy, the home of Art and intellect, felt that a rent had been made in the earth's diadem of mind. Charles I. of England had loved Rubens. On him the news fell like a blow, and deepened the darkness that was gathering round the doomed King.

The monument of Rubens is in all places where are pictures by his hand, or engravings of them, that speak to the heart and the intellect of his fellowmen. As a special memorial his widow erected, in the church of St. James in Antwerp a chapel, where, overhung by one of his best works, — a family-picture, with his wives, and children, and parents in it, and himself under the figure of St. George, — repose his remains. They consecrate this chapel as one of the holiest shrines of Europe, whither pilgrimages are made from all countries of Christendom by admirers of genius.

Inscribed on the monument in the chapel, and written by Gevaerts, the learned friend and nephew of Rubens, is an epitaph in Latin, of which this is a translation : —

"Here lies Peter Paul Rubens, knight, and lord of Steen, son of John Rubens a senator of this city. Gifted with marvelous talents, versed in ancient history, a master of all the liberal arts, and of the elegancies of life, he deserved to be called the Appelles of his age and of all ages. He won for himself the good will of monarchs and of princely men. Philip IV., King of Spain and the Indies, appointed him secretary of his Privy Council, and sent him on an embassy to the King of England in 1629, when he happily laid the foundations of the peace that was soon concluded between those two sovereigns. He died in the year of salvation 1640, on the 30th of May, aged sixty-three years."

Besides countless heirs of his soul, Rubens left heirs of his body ; and numerous descendants survive, some in Europe, and some in America. One of these is thankful that in his earlier years he had opportunities which, now in his later, empower him to write, and offer to readers on the American side of the Atlantic, the life of an illustrious man, of a man preëminent in a high calling, of one who was, and is, a benefactor to his kind, of PETER PAUL RUBENS.